THE LIGHT AT FINNIGAN'S END

RUM RUNNERS, BOOK 2

JODI GALLEGOS

To anyone who's ever had a dream...or a plan for retribution

A shudder crept up my spine as I inspected my new— *temporary*—home. I forced a smile as I pivoted to peek through the front window at the vast expanse of Lake Salvador. It was the furthest south I'd been since arriving in Jefferson Parish.

There was nothing special about the cabin. Two main rooms held the essentials. The walls were intact and the floor sturdy. Fresh bedding had been left for me in the splintered wardrobe.

"It ain't nothin' like you had in N'awlins, I'm sure. But it's private." Jack stepped behind me, grazing my backside. He leaned over my shoulder as if looking out the window. An unhealthy gray colored his sparse, once-brown curls. His pallor was that of a man who rarely spent time in the sun, clinging instead to the night. Only the bright veins of alcoholism spidering across his nose provided color.

The lecherous insinuation in his voice disgusted me only slightly more than his pronunciation of New Orleans.

"It'll be fine."

His breath warmed my neck, making the stale air feel oppressive.

I slipped away from him to inspect the other room.

In the kitchen, a dust-covered table and four mismatched chairs were pushed against built-in shelving. Haphazardly nailed scrap lumber formed shelves, each a different width and thickness. Some bowed up, and others down.

It makes no matter, I reminded myself. *They'll do just fine for the time they're needed.*

I crossed the kitchen and tugged on the door three times before it sprang free and opened onto a narrow-covered porch. Two wooden chairs, weathered and long abandoned, leaned against the exterior wall.

Lush greenery surrounded the back of the old fish camp. Thick palmetto leaves danced about the trunks of cypress and elm trees. Chartreuse colored moss dangled from above, taunting me to reach for it. The deep green of the bayou comforted my soul. It was warm and lovely, but it'd never be home. It wasn't Ireland. Despite my yearning, it seemed I'd never be able to leave Louisiana. I'd never again travel the road to where my forefathers' land ended, and the sea began. It was likely I'd die here, and my death was fast approaching.

Jack stepped beside me, wringing his hat in his hands, like a school boy waiting for the attention of a pretty classmate. But Jack Moret was no school boy. He was the brother of Claude Moret, and both were the most vicious hooligans I'd ever come across.

I forced a smile and hoped it appeared genuine. "Thank you again for your kindness. I don't know what I'd have done without your help." I caste my gaze up, lowered my lids ever so slightly, and then met his rheumy eyes again. "I'd have become destitute for certain."

He leaned toward me, lowering his head toward my own.

With a pronounced inhalation, he drew in my scent as an animal smells his prey on the breeze.

I stepped away and willed a blush to stain my cheeks before I hurried back into the cabin. *Innocent and demure,* I counseled myself. *Play the part.*

Jack followed me into the kitchen and leaned against the cupboard as I pulled several jars from my bag.

"I s'pose I should prepare. There hasn't been a traiteur in the area for quite a while. The people must have a long list of ailments they'll need tended to. I'm certain to be kept quite busy." My message was as indirect as it was clear. As a healer in an isolated community, I'd be busy. I'd have no time for Jack Moret to woo me.

"I'll stop by in a few days to check on ya'." He strode through the front door with the air of a man accustomed to being trailed by his subordinates.

I fell into my own role, following him down the porch steps and to the shoreline. Stepping carefully, I avoided the gaps in the dock where boards were missing. I couldn't risk falling through and breaking an ankle.

One of Jack's men waited next to my few belongings. I'd brought two cases: a small one of clothing and blankets, the other full of remedies. Jack lit a cigarette and nodded. The man picked them up and carried them into the cabin.

"In the meantime, I'll have some of my boys come by and check on ya. If anyone gives ya trouble, you tell 'em you're a guest of Claude Moret."

I nodded. "Thank you, Mr. Moret."

He edged closer, his large frame nearly blocking out the sun. With the hand that held his cigarette, he reached and lightly tugged at a red curl that had blown loose from my bobby pins. He tucked the strand behind my ear. The tips of his fingers lingered softly on my jawline as he pulled back and took a deep drag on his cigarette.

When he exhaled, my nose threatened to wrinkle at the stench. Jack leaned closer and dropped his voice to a smooth murmur. "I thought we agreed you'd call me Jack."

I gifted him with a smile as full of innocence as I could muster. After all, that's the persona that had lulled him into trusting me this far. To Jack I was an innocent Irish immigrant, without family, desperate to survive the financial collapse spreading across the country. He failed to realize that I was no simple immigrant, but a woman with nothing left to lose. I'd just as happily destroy myself if it meant successfully bringing Jack Moret, his brother and the rest of their gang to their knees.

"Of course, Jack. Thank you."

His gaze lingered on my face then his eyes dropped to my chest before he turned his attention back to the skiff. His man was waiting to push away from the splintered dock.

Jack nodded then turned and stepped into the boat. He fixed his gaze up the bayou as the man maneuvered the boat into the current. He was done with me and moving on to important business. *Moret* business. He wouldn't waste a moment to cast a glance back at the girl he was trying so desperately to seduce.

Your wife is such *a lucky woman.* Bitterness constricted my throat as I watched him disappear around the bend. I thought of the woman who was sitting home waiting for the attention of her criminal and philandering husband. *Certainly, I'm not the only woman he's tried to entice.* A man like Jack Moret went after, and often took what—and who—he wanted.

How would he respond when his attentions toward me failed? The steel blade pressing against my thigh reminded me that I knew the risks of taunting—and denying—Jack Moret.

For the remainder of the morning, I busied myself unpacking my meager belongings.

The sun warmed the small cabin as the hours passed toward noon. A slow, but heavy breeze floated through the open windows. The air was fresh but did little to cool the rooms.

I was grateful for the overgrowth of trees. Shade protected the cabin from direct sunlight during the early part of the day. The afternoon would be nearly intolerable though. Once the sun peaked over the trees, there'd be no relief until it set again. I imagined the back porch had been built to avoid the late-day sunlight.

The front room of the cabin faced the lake. It contained a bed, arm chair, small table and the old wardrobe. I'd utilize this room for my private living area. The kitchen, with the shelves, table and basin, would be ideal for treating patients and mixing remedies.

Outdoors, I found a cypress cistern and a bucket for hauling water. With my herbs and ointments placed on the shelves, my clothing and books unpacked, I poured water into the basin and washed the sticky sweat from my arms and neck. My hot skin prickled against the cool path of the wet rag. Goose pimples erupted along my arms at the sudden chilling, then melted away as the hot air exerted its dominant effect. It didn't seem possible that the humidity could be so much thicker in Cleric's Cove than in New Orleans. I doubted I'd ever adapt to the heavy, oppressive heat of Louisiana. I missed the cooler and lighter Irish air.

I'd have no better luck washing away the sticky film on my skin than removing the dark stain of vengeance that clouded my soul. Giving up, I returned to the wardrobe and pulled Mum's brocade carpet bag from the bottom. The material was thin, and the corners frayed. The metal clasp had the dark patina of three generations of use and resisted as I pushed it open. Once cream-colored, the satin liner was stained and rough.

I slid my hand into the hidden pocket. My fingertips pinched the links of my necklace and I pulled it into my palm. Throwing the bag back into the wardrobe I sat in the armchair, legs tucked under me, and looked out the front door at the lake. The water undulated, sunlight sparkling on each wave as they crested and fell again. The *woosh* of the swells as they lapped against the shore lulled me into tranquility.

I held the necklace tight to my chest, and the cool metal locket seemed to meld with my palm. My mind drifted, dwelling in images of the past. Mam, Da, Finnigan and I during happier times. Before we'd left Ireland. The possibility we'd dreamed of when we'd moved to New Orleans. Mam and Da setting up their practice and working together each day. Finn and I learning the arts of healing that'd been passed between every generation of Cassidy.

But those memories were before. Before Da got sick. Before the stock market crashed and jobs became harder to find. Before Finn turned to illegal activities—and the Morets—to help save our house.

I opened my palm and my fingers traveled across the dips and valleys of the design on the metal disk. I pushed my thumbnail into the groove on the side and opened the locket. My thumb fell into the empty divet that once held the last image of my happy family. The photo was gone now. Burned in a barrel fire on the banks of the Mississippi river. I'd had no choice. I couldn't risk anyone seeing that photo. If anyone from Cleric's Cove—or the Morets—were to see it and recognize Finn, then I'd lose the element of surprise. If anyone knew that Finn was my brother, it'd be harder for me to find out what happened to him. And harder for me to kill Claude Moret, if he had, indeed, killed my brother.

TWO

Whispers from outside pulled me from my memories. The delicate titter of giggles followed on the breeze. I set the locket on the small, wobbly table beside the chair and crept to the window.

A shuffle below, followed by a "*Ssh,*" indicated the direct location of my intruders. I crouched low and slinked toward the door. Reaching the frame, I pressed myself against it and pivoted onto the porch. My bare feet allowed me to navigate the boards without a sound. I eased myself onto an old stool and positioned to face the encroaching spies.

The whispers grew more intense as they neared. Three tufts of dark hair rose above the edge of the porch, followed by three pairs of charcoal eyes and three equally surprised gasps. All three children ducked back below the deck in an instant.

"Are ye spying on me or 'ave ye come to welcome me?" I smiled. It wouldn't do for them to be afraid of me. If I was to be the traiteur, the residents—children as well as adults—would need to feel safe coming to me. They had to know I wasn't a threat—to them anyway.

One pillow of black hair slowly rose again, followed by the

eyes and rounded cheeks of a girl. I guessed her to be six years old. She wrung her hands at her belly as if she'd been caught in the act of mischief.

"Hello there," I said. "I'm Deirdre. What's yer name?"

She swayed and tipped her head, eyes fixed on the ground. One rotund hand gripped the wrist of her other arm and she pointed one toe in front of her to trace a line in the soil. "My name's Odelia. But ev'ryone calls me Odi."

A chubby arm reached up and tried to pull her back into hiding.

Odi swatted at it. "Does Mr. Jack know you livin' in his hideout?"

Hideout? I didn't realize this cabin was a hideout. I'd assumed it was a fish camp like the others I'd seen and heard about. "Well, Odi, Mr. Moret was kind enough to let me stay here. He said ye could use a nurse in the area. That yer doctor left a year ago."

"Doc Sparks." Odi confirmed. "He disappeared. Ain't nobody knows where he went."

I have no doubt about that, I thought. *That's how Finn went missing.* "Well, I'm a nurse. If anybody needs help ye can send them to me."

"You talk funny," Odi said.

I laughed at her forthrightness. I leaned forward, resting my forearms on my knees. "I'm sure I do sound funny to you. But where I'm from everyone talks like this. Have ye ever heard anyone speak like I do?" It was a subtle question, I almost felt guilty for interrogating a child. But if she'd heard an Irish accent before, it could have been Finn's.

Odi shook her head and my spirits dropped.

"Where you from?"

"I was born far away. Across the ocean, in Ireland. Have ye heard of it?"

Odi nodded, but still seemed cautious, or perhaps curious, about me.

I leaned back on the stool, my back against the wall. "You know, Odi. I believe I might have packed a few bits of candy in my bags when I came. Would you like a piece?"

Two other heads popped up from under the edge of the porch. They had the same dark eyes and round cheeks as Odi, though they were both younger.

All three nodded. "Yes, Ma'am."

I went into the cabin and pulled three butterscotch bits from the bowl I'd placed on a high shelf. My fingers lingered in the candy dish tempted to pull out a few pieces more, but I imagined I'd be seeing a lot of these three. It'd be best to ration their sweets.

I handed them each a piece of candy along with a warning. "Now, all three of ye leave those in yer hand until you get home and ask yer mum if you can eat them. I won't be accused of ruinin' yer supper. If ye don't mind, you'll get no more sweets from me."

"Yes, ma'am." They each palmed their candy and sprinted off along the narrow path that led into the overgrowth. I hoped they'd do as told. It wouldn't do any good to make a mother mad on my first day in Cleric's Cove.

Across the lake, the sun settled low in the western sky. The orange glow of daylight melted into the encroaching lavender of early evening. A few crickets braved the twilight to share their nocturnal chorus. Bullfrogs joined in as the sky turned a deep indigo. A chill drifted in from Lake Salvador and goose-bumps prickled along my arms.

I reluctantly turned into the front room, closing the door on the nighttime symphony. My emerald colored shawl hung from the wardrobe. I pulled it across my shoulders as I made my way to the kitchen. My muscles were weighted with the exhaustion of the day and anticipation of all that still lie ahead for me in the bayou. Too tired to think about a full meal, I opened a can of potted hash and set it on the stove to heat.

With my shawl pulled tight around my shoulders, I returned to the stool on the front porch.

The tide crested and rolled under the light of the rising moon. A feeling of awe settled over me. I'd accomplished the first stage in my hastily organized plan. Despite the odds, I'd approached Jack Moret in the streets of New Orleans, gained his interest, and been brought into his fold. I'd be serving as nurse to Moret's men and the people he hid amongst.

Somewhere nearby, members of the Moret gang were sitting down to their suppers. Some had families of their own, perhaps their children were playing at their feet. Others were in the bayous, and the nearby towns, threatening—or even hurting—people on behalf of Claude Moret. I tried to stop my thoughts from picturing those situations, because inevitably, my imagination would get away from me and I'd see Finn at the hands of the Morets.

Finn, his fair red curls disheveled as faceless men accosted him. The freckles on his pale face mingling with specks of blood. His blue eyes distorted and swollen because of a Moret lackey. I snapped out of the horrible vision my mind concocted.

You don't know what's happened to him, I reminded myself. I willed rational thought to take over. But so long as my brother's fate remained unknown, I drifted further into the dark pit of an even darker path.

Our last conversation haunted my mind, the night Finn stood in the darkened hall and told me he was leaving.

"Ye can't go. Ye can't get be involved in their nonsense anymore."

"I don't have a choice, Dearey. Mr. Moret needs—"

"*We* need ye. Mam and Da." My hushed voice grew louder.

Though I hadn't recognized it at the time, a cloud of impending doom was blossoming in my chest, its fingers reaching into the depths of my being.

"I'm *doin'* this fer Mam and Da. And if ye can't see that—" He shook his head as he closed his bedroom door behind him.

The next morning, for the promise of a dollar, he walked out of our house and into the clutches of the Morets.

The longer he was gone, the more convinced I became that he wouldn't be back. And, if Finn wasn't able to return to his family, neither would the Moret who'd sealed his fate.

I forced another image into its place. Claude Moret—or Jack—gazing up at me, trust in his eyes, as I pulled a trigger. It was that image that carried me through my first night alone in the belly of the beast that was Moret's territory.

THREE

APRIL 6, 1930

Word of my arrival spread through the night. As the sky lightened, people showed up at the back door with a variety of ailments. Most were easily treated.

Odi had acquired a splinter in her great toe and refused to let her mum pull it out.

"I ain't happy 'bout takin' up your time, but she ain't lettin' nobody, but the new traiteur, touch that thing."

Odi sat in the chair, holding her foot up.

Her mother leaned closer to me, dropped her voice and let me in on Odi's secret. "I think she's only lookin' fer another bit of candy."

I couldn't help but laugh at the calculated nature of my small patient. I sat on a stool in front of her and lifted her foot onto my lap. "Well, let's just make sure we don't have to amputate it first."

Odi's mother and I both laughed at the girl's surprise before we assured her it was a joke.

The splinter was a fair size and I extracted it easily. Odi hissed as I dabbed witch hazel on the site.

"Now ye keep that clean for a day or two," I instructed. "And ye listen to yer mum, ye hear?"

"Yes'm." Odi slid from the chair and palmed the piece of candy I slid into her hand.

"I'm sorry to bother ya'," Odi's mother said. "I got no money, but I brought this. Maybe it'll help?"

She pulled two jars of honey from the cloth bag that hung from her shoulder.

"Honey is wonderful," I told her. "I use it all the time. This is too much, though. I hardly did a thing."

I handed one of the jars back. From the years my dad worked as a doctor and my mam as a midwife, I understood that people took great pride in paying for their care. It was rude to deny them the satisfaction of paying even if they could little afford to let go of anything.

I held out my hand as she took the extra jar. "My name's Deirdre."

"Leonie." She shook my hand. "Welcome to Cleric's Cove. People 'round here can be a bit closed off, but if ya need anythin' feel free to come lookin' for me. Ev'ryone knows evr'yone else round here. Of course, ya can prob'ly follow Odi's footprints and candy wrappers and find me just as easy."

She sighed and raised her brows as she added, "Keep in mind, in Cleric's Cove ev'ryone knows ev'ryone's buis'ness too."

I put on a grateful—and I hoped innocent—smile as we walked to the porch. I hoped the people wouldn't assume the same thing I'd led Jack to believe: that if I wasn't already, I'd soon be Jack Moret's lover.

After several hours of tending to rashes, nausea, and two very nervous first-time mothers, the crowd outside my door dissipated. Someone had left a milk bottle filled with sweet tea in the shade of the porch. I filled a small jelly jar with the sweet liquid and carried it out to the dock.

Clouds covered the sun and a cool breeze floated from the lake. I eased myself onto the end of the dock and, after checking the water below for unwelcome lurking animals, I dipped my feet into the water.

My fear of alligators overtook me within seconds, and I lifted my feet up and crossed my legs in front of me. I closed my eyes, enjoying the more tolerable afternoon. The mild temperature, overcast sky, and the undulations of the water all seeped into my bones, and the tension melted from my body. I laid back on the dock, the uneven boards pressing into my back while the heat they'd absorbed radiated into my aching muscles.

The sound of the water lapping at the dock and rolling against the shore became louder in my head. It smothered all other sounds and carried me into a deep slumber.

Something drew my attention, pulling me from sleep. My ears reached for sound. Had there really been a small engine or did I imagine it? My lids lifted slightly, the sharpness of daylight invading my vision. I squinted against the light as I rolled onto my side and back into consciousness.

"I was afraid you was dead," a gruff voice called.

I lifted my hand to shade my eyes. A bateau coasted across the waves and angled alongside the dock. Two men sat in the boat. Both were young, in their early twenties I guessed. The one who maneuvered the boat, pulling it tight against the dock, had dark brown hair, mussed by the wind, or perhaps from days of inattention to hygiene. From the veins of dirt that streaked his fingers and the soil staining his clothes I figured the lack of hygiene to be the case.

His partner was the complete opposite. His clothing was faded, but clean. The light brown curls atop his head were streaked with blond, as if spun with sunshine itself. His skin was tanned and clean. He appeared to have two days of growth on his face, but it appeared intentional and not at all ragged.

He reached for the dock and his hands, though clean, were cut open and bruised about at the knuckles. Dried blood had spidered into the narrow grooves of his skin.

I gestured at his right hand. "That cut's near ta bein' infected."

"Well, that's why I'm here." He had the easy smile of a man without troubles.

It'd been a long time since I'd seen someone with such an easy manner, and I found myself mesmerized by him. In New Orleans the depression had instilled a desperate and cautious manner in the most joyous of people. The "laissez les bons temps rouler" lifestyle had given way to poverty and hopelessness. Even the children lost their zest for life when faced with the reality of hunger and disease.

But this man acted as though he'd never known a hungry day. Had he never felt the cold grip of desperation?

With the boat tied off, they stepped onto the dock. The one who'd spoken stood over me. He raised his brows.

It was only when he offered a hand that I realized I'd been sitting on the dock simply staring at him.

I reached for his hand and let him pull me up, shaking the sleep from my head as I tried to hide my embarrassment. "I'm sorry. I must've fallin' asleep. I'm still a bit rummy. Let's get ye inside and tend to yer injuries."

THEY BOTH FOLLOWED as I led them around the back of the cabin and up the steps to the kitchen door.

"Wait here, Joe," the curly-headed one commanded.

Joe pulled one of the wooden chairs into the shade. He groaned as he lowered his weight onto the chair. As he leaned back he dug into his shirt pocket and extracted a very bent cigarette. He didn't appear put out by the command to stay behind. It was apparent that he was accustomed to taking orders.

In the kitchen I pulled a chair for the other to sit in.

He didn't take the seat right away. He walked around the room, looking at the jars on my shelves while I gathered cotton, water, and the ointments I'd need to treat the cuts on his knuckles.

The honey Leonie had left was on the shelf. I decided to use that as well to stave off infection.

"Excuse me." I leaned in front of him to retrieve the honey. He didn't move aside, and I felt the heat from his body as I brushed against him. I turned to face him.

He stood unmoving and looked down at me. His eyes were the bright blue of a summer's day with the intensity of a jungle cat tracking its prey.

His lips were nearly the perfect cupid bow shape. Clara Bow, herself, would envy the exquisite perfection of this man's mouth.

My heart hammered against the confines of my ribs, trapping my breath in my chest. Heat rushed up my neck and colored my face. I knew enough of myself to know the bright red of my blush was glaringly evident against the dark freckles dusting my nose and cheeks.

One corner of his mouth pulled up in amusement.

I forced myself to turn away. I carried my armload to the table and laid them out, busying my hands to hide their shaking.

"Take a seat in either chair." I needed a few more seconds to shake off my unexpected fascination with him and resume my duties as a nurse. "Let's have a look at yer hands."

He pulled a chair for me to sit first and then sat in the chair beside me. His legs were long, and I had to pull my own chair closer to treat him.

I lifted his hand close to inspect the wounds. It was a patchwork of healthy skin and old scar tissue, which was prone to split open easier. The first three knuckles on his right hand were bruised, split and swollen. The knuckle of his middle finger was in the worst condition. I guessed the injuries to have occurred one to two days prior. Infection hadn't yet set in but was still a risk.

I held his hand as gently as possible while I palpated the back of it, along the bones to check for breaks. As I pressed, I glanced up to see if he would wince. He didn't. His gaze held mine steadily and intently.

"It doesn't hurt?" I was surprised that he'd shown no evidence of pain.

"It hurts," he answered. His eyes stayed focused on mine. He didn't seem concerned that I knew he was staring.

Heat crept up, warming my face again. "Let me see the other." I reached for his left hand. The damage to it was far less.

"What happened?" I didn't have to ask, it was more of a courtesy and a tactic. I'd learned it from my dad. Even if you had no doubts what was wrong with a patient, you gave them the chance to tell their story. Often, you would learn more about your patient from the story they told you, truth or not, than you could learn from the obvious nature of their problem.

Based on the injuries I guessed there had been a fight. This man was obviously right handed. The absence of any noticeable injuries indicated he'd likely won. The fact that he had no injuries to his face told me his opponent hadn't fought back—or hadn't had the chance to.

"Had a disagreement." He was calm. At no point did he tense or pull away from me. He was used to remaining cool under questioning.

I continued to inspect the back of his hand, applying pressure to various points along his wrist and moving the joints of his fingers. His hands were warm in my own. Aside from the scarring and the injuries at the knuckles, they were soft and smooth. I turned his hand over to inspect for other injury. His right hand had a deep scar across the palm. An obvious cut. My finger traced the length of the scar.

"What happened here?"

"It's old," he said simply. There was no reason for me to be concerned about the scar, and it was evident he had no desire to explain it.

He sat still while I cleaned his wounds.

While his skin dried, I mixed together a paste of charcoal, chamomile, comfrey and honey.

His brows pinched together when he saw the mixture.

"It looks terrible, but it'll reduce the inflammation and help prevent infection." I applied it liberally to the cuts then wrapped a bandage around his knuckles.

He wasn't likely to leave it on very long, but at least I'd done my due diligence in treating him.

"Leave them wrapped for the rest of the day. Come back if it they don't seem to be healing or if they turn red."

"They'll be fine. Always are." He stood.

Always, I thought. I knew based on the condition of his hands that this hadn't been his first fight. I wondered how many fights he'd been in. *Were they even fights?* There was a very real possibility these wounds were the result of attacks, not fair fights.

I stood, screwing the lids back on the jars and then and walked him toward the door.

Joe heard the door open and stood. He walked down the steps, onto the path and dropped his cigarette to the ground, grinding it into the damp soil with the heel of his boot.

"We'll be back tomorrow," my patient said. "I'm s'posed to check on ya ev'ry day. Make sure yer doin' okay."

Jack! This hadn't been a random visit from someone in need of medical attention. Jack Moret had sent one of his thugs to check on me. Maybe even to spy on me. Rage lit a slow burning fire in the pit of my belly.

I shook off my irritation and put on my kindest and most unaffected look. I couldn't allow Jack Moret or his associates to suspect I had anything to be suspicious of. "That's kind of you. I appreciate it. I'm Deirdre, by the way."

He reached for the hand I offered and shook it gently.

I was acutely aware of how close he was to me. Aware of the warmth of his hand and the energy he seemed to emit— and how silence hung in the air around him, waiting for something magical to happen.

His voice was low and smooth. "Pleased ta meet ya. I'm Claude Moret."

A gasp leapt into my chest before I could control my response. My brows pulled together as I stepped back to take in this stranger with new clarity. "Claude Moret? But, I thought —" I stammered like an idiot. "I thought you were. I mean, you're younger than—"

He laughed as I pulled my hand from his. My impulse was to wipe the tainted touch of Claude Moret from my hand immediately, but good sense took hold of me again.

"I'm Claude Moret, *Junior*," he clarified. "But don't call me that. Ev'ryone calls me Mo."

"Oh. Well, it's nice to meet ye, Mo." I was relieved, both that I'd finally regained my composure and that I wasn't standing face-to-face with the actual Claude Moret. As much as I'd imagined the meeting, I still wasn't entirely prepared to be standing across from the devil of the bayou.

I followed Mo around the corner of the cabin and watched

from the shore as he and Joe got back into their bateau. Mo pushed away from the dock, and Joe started the small engine.

Mo looked back over his shoulder as they pushed into tide. The corner of his mouth pulled up into a smile again. "I'll be seein' ya', Deirdre."

My heart thundered, but I couldn't tell if it was in response to the danger of having been so close to Claude Moret's son or the thrill of it.

I watched as they drifted along the shoreline. Just before they disappeared around the bend, Mo Moret turned and looked over his shoulder one last time.

CHAPTER

FOUR

Mo did return the next day, as well as the three following days. Each time a different person accompanied him and waited on the porch or at the dock.

I changed Mo's bandages and applied more ointment the first two days even though the wounds were healing nicely. The surge of electricity each time I touched his hands never dissipated. I still couldn't decide if it was fear, or something else, that caused it.

On the third day, without the dressing changes to ease us into conversation, things grew awkward. I wanted to know more about Mo Moret. I *needed* to know more about his father and Jack. It was my only way of getting to the truth about what happened to Finn.

"I made biscuits," I offered, stumbling for something to say. I was compelled to keep Mo around for longer than the few minutes it took him to ask if I needed anything. I reminded myself that it would be wise to have a secondary route into the Moret gang should I fail with Jack.

I prepared a pot of the steaming chicory coffee preferred by

21

so many of the men and set out two cups. I would join him, even though chicory—and coffee in general—was far stronger than I preferred.

"Have ye always lived in Cleric's Cove?" It always seemed easier to begin with nonsense talk. *Keep it conversational,* I reminded myself. *Nothing threatening or too intrusive.*

"Mostly." Mo pulled the chair from the table and sat. He poured coffee for each of us as I placed the biscuits on the table. I put a spoon in the honey and set that on the table as well—in case Mo Moret had a sweet tooth.

He did. He spooned honey onto his biscuit then he studied me, as if he wasn't sure why I was talking to him.

I was in the chair directly across the table from him.

Mo remained still, biscuit in one hand looking as if I might leap across the table and attack him.

I lifted my brows and smiled at him as I reached for my own biscuit and slathered honey across the steaming pillow. "It's called conversation, Mo. People string multiple words together as means of exchangin' pleasantries."

He cocked his head and smirked as he took a bite of his biscuit. "I know what conversation is. I'm just wonderin' why. In three days you hardly said a word to me. You ain't asked nothin' 'bout me or Cleric's Cove before. Why now?"

I decided that the truth—or some fraction of it—might be the best course. I sipped my coffee, the bitterness causing me to pucker as I swallowed. "It's a bit awkward, but while I was tendin' to yer wounds we had that to focus on. To talk about. Now that they're better, I'm at a loss for what to say when a man comes into me house ev'ry day."

Mo nodded as he chewed and then swallowed his bite. He sipped his own coffee and set the cup on the table before leaning back in his chair. He took a deep breath, wiping his hands on his pants. His intense blue eyes focused on mine. "I grew up in Cleric's Cove. I spend a lot of time in Jean Lafitte and Gretna. I don't really live anywhere, just stay a bunch a places. My dad is Claude Moret, and I got no more to say on that subject."

I dipped my spoon into the sugar bowl, added a second teaspoonful to my coffee, and stirred slowly. The coffee had cooled a bit, but the harsh flavor had not.

"And Jack Moret?" I asked.

Mo's cupid bow lips pulled into the devil's sneer. "Jack's my uncle. He brought ya here. And so long as you're sharin' his bed I imagin' I'll be forced to continue checkin' on ya."

I hadn't intended to fling the spoon at Mo. I didn't realize I even had until the droplets of coffee splattered across his face.

The spoon clattered as it hit wall and then fall to the floor.

As shocked as I was to have done that, I was even more enraged. I sprang up, the chair toppling behind me. I leaned on the table, furrowing my brows as I looked directly in Mo's eyes. "How dare you."

Mo sat calmly. Matching the challenge in my eyes with an unworried smirk. With one hand he reached up and wiped the droplets from his cheek then dried it on his pants. He cast a side gaze at me that was slightly amused but challenging. Daring me to go further.

My Irish brogue thickened with the heat of my anger. "I'll 'ave ye know, I'm no' sharin' a bed wit yer uncle. Nor wit any udder man. Now ye git ou' me 'ouse now, Mo Moret. An' do'n ye come back."

I turned and stormed from the cabin, slamming the door behind me. Fury propelled me deep into the overgrowth along the path. Though I had yet to walk that far, I knew the footpath led to the most populated section of Cleric's Cove.

The soil path was damp and well worn. Marshes lay on each side of the trail. The water didn't appear deep, but I knew they were deep enough for a small gator to hide in. *Or, worse yet, snakes!*

I hoped that with the amount of overgrowth and cooler weather of the past few days that it was too cool for gators and snakes to be a concern. Nevertheless, I maintained a fast pace and the utmost awareness for any movement.

The path ended in a clearing that bordered the lake. Several cabins lined the shoreline and spread into the tree line. A group of children, Odi and her cousins among them, played kick the can at the far edge of what seemed to be a common area. A swing hung from the limb of an oak tree.

I sat on the swing and swayed as I watched the kids run about. The exertion of the walk, and the joy of children at play, allayed the anger I'd carried in me.

As I calmed down I was able to think about things with a clearer mind. I couldn't be mad at Mo. He'd only assumed what had been implied: that I was Jack's lover. I shuddered in disgust at the thought of sharing a bed with Jack Moret. Also, at the idea that every person in Cleric's Cove most likely believed I was Jack's lover as well.

That isn't what matters, I chastised myself. I tried to rein in my emotions and let reason take over. *You'll do whatever it takes to find out what the Morets did to Finn and get revenge. What people believe about you is inconsequential.*

I *wanted* to get to know Mo, but more importantly, I *needed* to get to know him. It was possible that Mo had known Finn. And though I didn't want to believe it, it was also possible that Mo was involved in—or even responsible for—whatever they did to my brother.

My feelings about Mo were conflicted. There was something about him that I was drawn to. He seemed very different from Jack. He lacked the animalistic quality of a person who could turn on you at any moment. He didn't seem the kind of person to hurt someone else—without good cause.

Christ, Deirdre, you've known the boy four days! There was no way I had any idea of who—or what kind of person—Mo Moret was.

"Miss Deary," Odi and the other kids noticed me in the shade and ran over to greet me. I had no candy to offer today, but they were still happy to see me.

One of the boys tugged at my hand as he whispered, "Come see my brother. He's brand new."

They pushed and pulled at me until I rose from the swing. It was easy to be carried away in the joy of this merry band of children.

We walked as a group to a small, one room home. The other children peeked in the windows as little Beau led me in to see his mére.

She was a young girl, hardly a day older than myself. She held the baby to her breast, nursing him. The baby suckled easily, and the mother didn't appear to be in any pain.

"Hello," I called in a whispered voice.

She smiled at me and at Beau. "I didn't call for a traiteur. Had my mére and granmére to help with the baby," she said.

I sat on the chair next to her and patted her arm softly. "It looks like you've done fine on yer own. Beau wanted me to see his brother. He's quite proud. Are ye feelin' alright?"

She nodded. "Just tired."

"That's to be expected, then." I smiled. "He's quite beautiful. You'll have yer hands full when they get to runnin' around together."

She beamed at Beau who stroked the baby's cheek.

"I'll leave you to them. If ye do need anything, please let me know. I'm the nurse. I'm renting the cabin at the end of the path." It wasn't the truth, but I thought that each story of how

I'd come to be at the Moret cabin lessened the truth behind the most distasteful one.

I allowed the kids to lead me about for several hours. They showed me their favorite trees to climb, the best place to catch fresh crab and crawfish. We even sat on the dock and fished as the sun began it's slow decent toward the horizon. With only one small catfish taking the bite, we gave up, freeing our catch.

We walked along the edge of the lake and took up a collection of what seemed to be the perfect skipping stones. I found a rock that sparkled in the sun, and the children were convinced it contained gold. I pulled it from my pocket and laid it on a piece of drift wood. "The person who skips their stone the furthest gets to keep the gold."

They scampered eagerly, searching for even more rocks to increase their chances.

"Miss Deary look at mine."

"Miss Deary, this one's the best."

Each time one of them mispronounced my name, and the others adopted that moniker, my heart warmed a bit more.

Though my parents had named me Deirdre, for as long as I could remember, they'd only ever referred to me as Deary. There wasn't a person in County Meath who knew me as Deirdre Cassidy—only as Deary.

An impressive pile of stones accumulated at my feet. I insisted they divide the stones evenly so each of them would have an equal number of chances at the prize. A half-hour later, they'd only gone through half the rocks but were enjoying themselves so much I didn't dare rush them.

It was well past dark when I returned to my cabin. An older couple insisted on walking with me. They must have seen the fear in my eyes at the thought of walking into the dark alone.

With the door closed behind me, I searched the shelves for my matches. It was late, but I still needed to clean the kitchen before I turned in for the night. The biscuits and honey on the table would surely attract insects if I left them any longer.

The kitchen felt empty. Mo wasn't here and would likely—and thankfully—not be returning. Fury simmered low in my chest as I replayed his words in my mind. It was followed by embarrassment at how quickly I'd let a Moret get to me. I hadn't been in control of my emotions, and that could prove dangerous.

I scraped the match against the striking paper and the orange glow sparked to life. The wick of the candle caught quickly, and a soft glow filled the small room.

I set the candle on the counter next to the sink, nearly knocking over a coffee mug. I looked to the table and then back to the counter. Two cups, spoons and plates sat on a towel. The biscuit tin and coffee pot were also set out to dry. I picked them up and looked closely. There wasn't a single crumb or ground sticking to either. The table had been cleared and the honey jar was back on the shelf. Mo had cleaned up before he left.

Why would he do that? I'd yelled at him. I'd thrown a coffee covered spoon at him. Perhaps it was simply because he still believed me to be his uncle's lover, and he was expected to show a bit of respect.

Whether he was acting as was expected or because he simply wanted to be nice, I had to keep in mind that he was a Moret. He was as guilty as the rest of them. Even if it was only by association.

Lightning flashed across the darkness, splitting the sky as it passed.

I retrieved my necklace and secured it around my neck before climbing into the bed.

Laying on my side, I palmed the locket and allowed memories of my family to join me in the dark room.

"Shush, the two o' ye." Mam's voice was as clear as when we were children. As if she were still just through the doorway.

Finn and I used to lie face-to-face every night. We'd giggle and tell stories of the ridiculous things we'd seen during the day. The goal was to make each other laugh uncontrollably. The one who laughed loud enough to catch our mam's attention was the loser. Most times it was I who lost. It was a game I was always happy to cede to my brother.

"I swear ta Jaysus." Mam would curse as she finally threw open the door. "Ev'ry feckin' night with the two of yer. If ye can't shush up so we can sleep, I'll separate ye."

That always shut us up. We'd never dared to be separated. We'd come into the world together and were determined to go out the same way.

My eyes stung, and warm tears tumbled over my lashes. I wiped them away.

I wasn't ready to admit that Finn might be gone forever. Despite the vacancy that echoed in my heart—the one that whispered, *"He's gone, Deary"*—I could never give up on Finn. I had to know for sure.

If there was any chance that he was alive, I'd find him. I'd promised Mam and Da. It was a promise that I'd die to fulfill even though I'd no longer have to answer to them should I fail.

They were both gone now. The tuberculosis that claimed my father had taken Mam within days. Perhaps it was her heart that took Mam. She never said the words, but her eyes declared that she believed Finn to be long gone. With Da passing away so soon after, and the tuberculosis settling into her own lungs, she'd simply given up the fight. She'd lost so much. My parents never discovered what happened to Finn, and he had no idea of their fate either. Perhaps they'd all met up at the pearly gates, each surprised to see the next.

I closed my eyes again, forcing the image from our photo

into my head. The four of us at the beach just south of Bettystown with sunlight sparkling off the Irish Sea behind us. My parents had gone into town for supplies. They told us they had a bet that the sunrise wasn't near as beautiful in town as it was at the end of our own lane. There was a reason so many of our family lived along the same lane and continued to name their eldest boy after it. Finnigan's End was the most amazing and peaceful place on earth. The sunrise from the end of our quiet lane was unparalleled. Finn and I knew Bettystown couldn't compete, and it hadn't. We posed for a photo anyway, to commemorate our trip. It was the last one we'd taken before we'd left for the promise of America.

Though I'd come to love New Orleans, I'd never again experienced anything like the majesty of morning rising high above Finnigan's End.

I'd kept the locket tight about my neck as we'd sailed across the Atlantic and settled into our new life. When Finn went missing, and Da got sick, I pulled it out more often. I comforted myself in the hope that we would one day be joined again as we were in the picture. In the photo we were smiling, arms wrapped around each other's necks as if we'd never let go. As if we'd be together forever.

My eyes burned again. Tears found a path between my lids and onto the mattress. The image in my memory curled at the edges and bubbled, the same way the picture had. Before I could change my mind, before I could reach into the fire and snatch the memory into safety, it was gone. Blackened ash and darkness.

FIVE

APRIL 10 TO APRIL 12, 1930

The clouds that had been gathering in the sky over the past several days brought friends. Together, they opened up and poured their bounty in a heavy, relentless rain that woke me.

I loved it. I threw open the doors and windows to welcome the cool air into the cabin.

I put on the kettle, and while I waited for the water to boil, pushed the armchair through the front door and onto the porch. The porch was deep enough that I'd be able to sit in the chair without getting it—or myself—wet. With my cup of tea in hand and a heavy shawl pulled around my arms, I sat in the armchair and tucked my feet under me.

The day was silent except for the splatter of rain drops and the lapping of the water.

A morose mood had settled in last night and still hung over me. *It must have been the storm brewing.* How else had I fallen so quickly into sadness?

"Mornin'."

I nearly jumped from my skin at the voice. I snapped my head around and there, in my doorway, stood Mo Moret.

"Yer drippin' all over me floor," I chastised. Turning my attention back to the lake, I settled back and sipped from my mug. I silently commanded by muscles to relax and my lungs to draw in air, determined to not give Mo the pleasure of a reaction. Not again, anyhow. I just had to calm the damn thundering in my heart.

Mo stepped to the edge of the porch. As he tipped his hat brim, the water poured over the edge and onto the dirt below. Turning to face me, he reached into his pocket, leaned toward me and laid a small glass jar on my lap.

I glanced at it but didn't reach for it. "What's this?"

"Blackberry jam. My mére made it."

I stared at him. What the hell reason did he have for giving me jam?

Mo squatted, the hat in his hand. He shook his head slightly while he searched for the words. "I'm sorry 'bout yesterday. I didn't mean to offend you."

I wanted to yell at him. Wanted to scream my indignation at him, but I also wanted to know what he had to say.

"I thought—," he stammered. "I mean, I assumed…"

"Maybe ye shouldn't have," I interrupted.

"You're right. I shouldn't have." He'd run out of things to say but was searching for a reason to stay. "That coffee?"

"Tea." I sipped from my mug but didn't offer him any.

"I like tea," he said, thick with expectation.

"Then perhaps you should go in and make yerself a cup." I sipped from my own mug again.

A slow smile pulled at Mo's lips and he stood. He dropped his hat on the old stool and removed his jacket, draping it over a nail in the side of the house. He headed to the door.

"Don't you wear yer wet boots in my house," I warned.

"Yes, ma'am." He kicked the boots off and lined them evenly just outside the door.

I heard the clatter as he put the kettle on. There was more shuffling from the back room, but I wasn't about to turn and have him think I found any interest in what he was doing.

A light scraping sound was followed by a bump as Mo dragged my small side table onto the porch.

I glared up at him.

He went back into the house and returned a few moments later with tea towel. He laid it across the table before disappearing back into my house.

"What the devil are ye up to, Mo Moret?"

This time he appeared with an armful. He unwrapped the biscuits from yesterday's batch and placed them on a plate. He set the honey down and reached for the jam, opening it as well before placing a spoon in it.

The kettle whistled, and Mo returned with two steaming cups of tea. "I thought yours might be cool. Thought you'd like a hot cup."

The fluttering in my chest was hard to contain. *There's no way this man is a Moret,* I chastised myself.

Oh, but he is, my better sense chimed in. *And you'd do best to not lose sight of that.* I'd uncovered far too many stories about the Morets, and not one ended with any demonstration of kindness.

Mo looked around the porch for a place to sit.

I sighed. "You should pull out a chair from the kitchen."

Before I knew it, Mo not only had a chair on the front porch but positioned right next to me.

He reached for a biscuit. His grip was gentle as he pulled it apart and laid the top aside. He dug a spoonful of jam from the jar and smeared the black jelly in a thick layer on the biscuit. "I really am sorry 'bout yesterday. I was an ass."

I wanted to tell him that I was sure it was Jack who had put that thought in his head, but I didn't dare say a word against his family. Being in Jack Moret's world, even on the periphery of it, was my only hope of finding Finn. "I'm sure there are rumors 'bout how I came to be here. Why I'm livin' in a Moret hideout."

"You mean fishing camp. Who said it was a hideout?" His question was smooth and cool. The unsurprised reaction of someone who'd grown up being cautious of every word he uttered.

"Perhaps the same people who said I'm sleepin' with yer uncle?"

Mo laughed. It was a genuine and infectious laugh. "Them people have a lot to say, I'm afraid."

We ate in silence. Sipping our tea as we watched the rain fall.

"Do you know why they named this Cleric's Cove?"

"No." I'd never even wondered, but now I found myself eager to hear the answer. Eager to hear Mo talk about something other than his family. And blackberry jelly.

"Goes back to the pirate days. Jean and Pierre Lafitte, and the likes. The privateers decided that if the people were calling a place something like Buccaneer's Bay, or Pirate's Cove, it'd be a sure clue to bounty seekers that pirates traveled through that place. The inlet that lets into the bayou from here was well hidden. It leads clear up north to N'Orleans. From this cove there's always a channel somewhere that's open all the way to the Mississippi. But privateers didn't want anyone else to find out about it, so they named it Cleric's Cove and paid the locals to start callin' it the same. They even brought in a bunch of priests and set up a seminary. Nobody huntin' a bounty is about to disrupt the studies of a group of holy men. So, Cleric's Cove hides a major route from Lake Salvador to N'Orleans."

I marveled at the fact that Cleric's Cove had been a trade route for pirates so many years ago and still served as major route for illegal activities like the Morets' bootlegging operation. After Finn went missing, I ran into an old friend of his at the St. Roch Market. From him I discovered Finn had not only been selling stolen merchandise, but also running moonshine from Jefferson Parish into New Orleans with a boy named Tulley Bishop.

It was Jack who'd inadvertently let me know that the Morets had "business" in Plaquemines Parish as well. He took me to dinner one night and, after several whiskeys, mentioned he was leaving in the morning for some business in Point de Concession and Belle Chaise.

"That's a far more interesting story than the one of my home," I said. I was caught between images of Mo's story and memories of the place I'd come from. I couldn't let Mo know that I was studying his story, filing it away with all the other details I knew about his family. I had to be as seemingly open with him as I'd been with Jack. It was time for me to put on my wistful Irish immigrant persona again. Time to reel in another Moret.

Mo set his empty cup on the table and turned toward me. "Tell me," he said.

"It's silly and simple really. My great-great-great-great grandfather set off to find a place he'd dreamt about. He walked across Ireland for months. He crisscrossed from the Atlantic Ocean to the Irish Sea. On his final night he'd become so weary that he realized he might never find the place he'd dreamed of. He decided to walk through the night and wherever he found himself when the sun rose was where he'd stop."

I set my own cup aside. I felt silly telling the story out loud. I'd heard the family legend since my youngest days and had always taken it as fact. Now, saying it out loud, I realized how similar to a fable it was.

Just as I was about to wave away the rest of the story, Mo

leaned forward, expectation lifting his brows and pushing a smile onto his lips.

"He found himself surrounded by thick trees. As the sky lightened, the small path he'd been following ended. As the sun peaked over the horizon, it cast an orange glow that glistened between the spaces in the trees and onto the rocky cliff below. It was the most beautiful sunrise he'd ever seen and, as he looked about, he recognized the lane as the one he'd dreamed of. He settled right there, overlookin' the ocean where Ireland ended, and the sea began. There isn't a family there now that isn't some relation to him."

I laughed at how ridiculous our familial heritage must seem to someone who'd been born and raised in America. "To this day, the lane bears his name and the first-born son of nearly every family is named after it. Even me own brother."

"What's it called?"

My breath caught in my chest and my heart thundered. I'd nearly made a catastrophic error. There was no way I could tell Mo my brother's name. I focused on brushing away non-existent crumbs from my lap. "What?"

"The road you grew up on. What's it called?"

Finnigan's End, my mind screamed, curious to see if he'd make the connection. "It's, uh, Connall's End." I substituted in the name of my dad—the second born son in his own family.

"Connall's End." Mo repeated the name as he looked back toward the churning lake. "I like it."

"As do we." I smiled and stood. Picking up our cups and biscuit plate, I avoided any further personal revelations on my part.

Mo gathered the honey, jam, and tea towel. He carried them into kitchen and, without a word, rinsed the cups and plate.

We bustled about the kitchen in comfortable silence until the clean-up was complete. Mo returned the small table to front room and pulled my armchair just inside the door. "You can still look out if ya want, but you should stay outta the rain. If ya catch a chill and get sick, you ain't gonna be no help to anyone else."

"That's probably a good idea. I just hate to miss the cool temperature."

An awkward silence descended again.

"I'd better head on out." Mo walked to the front door. He bent to step into his boots, then he pulled on his jacket.

I wanted to invite him to stay and visit.

"I got some business to take care of," he said. "My père ain't gonna wait on me all day. Rain or shine, business needs done."

The business he referred to was Moret business. I reminded my ridiculous heart that despite how charming Mo might be, he was a Moret. He worked for Claude and Jack Moret. That made him just as guilty as either of them might be.

I gazed at his knuckles. They were no longer wrapped in gauze, and the skin was now pulled taut with scab formation. The thought crossed my mind, for the first time, that Mo Moret may have very well carried out a sentence against Finn on behalf of his father or his uncle.

Mo slid the hat onto his head as he stepped through the door. He turned as he reached the edge of the porch.

My heart lunged forward, wanting to step closer, to watch Mo as he walked away. I was compelled to say something to him. To gaze up into his blue eyes. But the steely anger in my core rose up to drive away my heart's inclinations. I pulled my shawl about me and straightened my spine. "Well, goodbye then, Mr. Moret."

I turned and closed the door behind me without a glance out the windows, even though I saw his figure pass them from the corner of my eye.

SIX

APRIL 13, 1930

obody came for care that day. Nor the next. The heavy rains had driven everyone to stay indoors.

I was locked away with nothing but my desperation to find some clue about Finn and my dark desire to make some progress in my vengeance upon the Morets. Every person I'd questioned so far had skillfully avoided giving me any information about the Morets. I was closer than ever to the Morets, how could I be so far from the answers I sought?

Early the following morning, hours before the sun was due to rise, I was awoken by shouting.

I leapt from my bed and scrambled to light a candle. Fear rose in my throat, constricting my ability to breath. The fact that I was alone and quite removed from the populace of Cleric's Cove—and any sort of help—became glaringly apparent. If I was in danger, there was nothing I could do.

I scrambled for my blade and hurriedly secured it around my thigh under my nightgown. I pulled my shawl around me and listened at the door. I tried to control the sound of my breathing, so my ears could better pick up the sounds from outside.

"Damn it," a man's voice yelled.

A groan filled the air followed by mumbled words of several men.

"Deirdre, open the door," a voice yelled. I didn't recognize it.

The heavy stomping of boots thundered on the front porch.

I rushed to open the door, turning the handle just as it was flung aside, and a large man pushed past me. His face was tanned and leathered, and he cast me an irritated look. Leaving a path of muddy footprints, he walked into the kitchen.

The sounds of moaning and men bickering drew my attention back to the porch. Three men carried another. The groans of the man being carried grew. His shadowed form writhed as he bounced in the air, suspended in the hands of his comrades.

I scooted to the side of the room, against the wall, as they clattered onto the porch and through the door. They deposited the man firmly onto my bed.

I heard the door close and turned to see Jack Moret standing beside me.

"No coffee?" The first man, grizzled in appearance, dripping and standing in my kitchen, looked expectantly at me.

By the curl and color of his dark, but graying hair, the thick brows and fierce look, I knew this was Jack's brother. Claude Moret had just walked into my house—his house actually— in the middle of the night. And carrying a bloody man. Somehow, I assumed this wasn't an uncommon turn of events in their sphere.

I was unsure whether to tend to the man who was clutching his belly and bleeding on my bed or brew Claude Moret coffee.

"Hey," Mr. Moret snapped his fingers in my direction. "Coffee."

And thus, the decision was made for me.

As I walked through the narrow doorway into the kitchen, I

was forced to turn and nearly press myself into the door jamb to get past him.

He made no effort to step aside to make room for me.

I filled the kettle and put it on to boil.

"Mo, get out there and drag in the boats," Claude gruffed. "Make sure they're hidden."

I tried to not whirl around. With all the men wearing hats, plus the writhing and bloody man, I hadn't noticed that Mo was among them. Also, I knew it would do no good to give any sort of reaction to Mo with Jack Moret standing in the next room.

With the water heating, I turned my attention to the man lying in—and bleeding all over—my bed. His eyes were wide and desperate. Tears accumulated on his lower lashes, though it was evident he was trying to not shed them. He was doing his best to maintain the demeanor of a man who, although in pain, was stoic and worthy of Claude Moret's trust.

"Lemme have a look." I met his eyes, trying to portray calm and understanding.

His hands clutched firmly just above his umbilicus.

I laid my hands on his hips, applying a gentle pressure. "What's yer name?"

He didn't answer. He rolled his gaze from me and moaned again before his eyes focused on Claude standing across the room. The vision of Claude Moret seemed to infuse him with stoicism again. "Joseph," he said.

"Joseph, I need to have a look." I pulled again at his hands, and he finally relented, letting me pull them aside.

I lifted the hem of his shirt. Dark burgundy blood oozed from a puncture. The wound was jagged, I imagined the blade that created it hadn't been terribly sharp and had torn its way into his flesh, rather than causing a clean slice.

"Okay, Joseph. I'm gonna need to feel around a bit. It might cause ye some discomfort."

His gaze fell on his boss again, but he nodded in agreement and winced in preparation of the pain to come.

I palpated his abdomen and around the wound. Joseph tensed his abdominal muscles against the pressure of my hands but didn't pull away. As I pressed around the immediate area of the wound, I made note of the quality and consistency of the fluid that seeped from the opening while also visualizing the tissue inside the wound. The fluid was thick and red. The metallic aroma of blood wafted about me as I assessed him. The absence of obvious gastrointestinal fluid was encouraging. I was hopeful that only his skin and muscles had been punctured. Any gastrointestinal injury was far more serious than I could care for, and I was certain that there was no way poor Joseph would ever be taken to a hospital. I would be the only medical attention he'd receive.

Mo entered the cabin while I was tending to Joseph. From my peripheral vision I saw that he went into the kitchen and finished the coffee. He presented his father with a steaming mug.

"Get me a towel from the kitchen," I ordered one of the men who leaned against the wall, watching me work. He returned quickly, and I pressed the towel into Joseph's belly and guided his hands to hold it in place. I stood and faced Jack.

"I'll need to clean the wound and bind it. I can make an ointment that'll hopefully prevent infection from setting in. But he won't be able to be up and about for several weeks."

Jack nodded.

"He'll stay here then." Claude stepped in front of Jack. He was not only commanding my attention but making it evident that it was he who I was to address. Claude Moret was in charge.

My stomach roiled in loathing for this man.

"I only have the one bed," I explained. Certainly, Joseph had his own home to go to.

"And it'll be just fine for him." Claude turned and went into the kitchen. I heard the strike of a match and smelled the bitter-sweet scent of cigar smoke. A chair scraped across the wood floor and then Claude beckoned his men. "Mo! Jack! Get in here."

They both hustled into the kitchen without pause and sat at the table with Claude.

"I'll be right back," I whispered to Joseph. "I have to get some supplies."

I kept my head down as I stepped into the kitchen, so it would be apparent that my intention wasn't to eavesdrop.

"Excuse me. I need to gather a few items."

From the shelves I pulled down a few rags for cleaning, a bowl for water and small jar of moonshine. It would hurt like hell when I rinse the wound with it, but I couldn't imagine anything with a higher content of alcohol. It was the only thing in my supplies that would provide a decent cleaning of Joseph's wound. I also pulled down the charcoal, yarrow and cayenne that I'd ground into a poultice just the other day. With my entire stock of bandages added to the pile I carried my supplies into the front room.

"Get me another cup, boy," Claude commanded—passing his cup to Mo— as I walked from the kitchen.

Mo quickly rose and filled his father's cup.

They didn't resume talking amongst themselves until I left the room.

Joseph tried to remain stoic as I cleaned his wound. Although he didn't cry out, he writhed in silent agony when I rinsed the wound with the liquor.

One of the men standing against the wall began to waver

and sway. His color had gone quite pallid, and his eyes became fixed to the floor.

"Perhaps ye should help yer friend into the chair," I told the other man who had found an unflinching fascination in my wound care.

"Oh. Yeah." He smacked his mate on the arm and nudged him toward the chair.

"Thanks," the man said and collapsed into the chair. He shook his head as if shaking off a trance and took a deep breath.

I laughed in my head. A scruffy hooligan, a ruffian as we called them in Ireland, nearly laid out by the sight of blood. *Not so tough after all, are ye?*

Once Joseph's wound was cleaned and wrapped, I administered several solid gulps of the illegal liquor to him. "I'm afraid it's all I've got to offer ye."

He was asleep in minutes. The shock of the initial injury compiled with the travel to my cabin and the arduous process of assessing, cleaning and binding his wound had left him exhausted.

The man in the chair had resumed a more natural color as well. He leaned back in the chair, eyes closed and mouth slightly agape. His breathing was deep and loud.

The other man had lowered himself to the floor, arms resting on his knees, head against the wall as he too slept.

Murmurs continued from the kitchen as the yellow glow of sunshine cast through the windows, and the sky outside brightened.

I cleared my throat before stepping into the kitchen.

Three identical pairs of eyes looked at me expectantly. "I think he'll be alright. It seems that only the muscle was cut, though I can't be completely certain. I have plenty of remedies on hand. I've used the last of me bandages. I'll need more if I'm to keep tending to him."

On impulse I decided to push my luck. "I could use another jar of whiskey as well. And some proper rubbing alcohol."

Both Jack and Mo cast a surprised look to Claude. Moonshine was liquid gold in this area, and the Morets were gold miners.

Claude held my gaze.

I stood firm, but not defiant. I wanted him to know this was a nonnegotiable need. If Joseph was valuable to the Moret gang, and I assumed he was or they wouldn't have brought him to me, then they'd do what was necessary to ensure he could return to them.

Claude nodded. "Take care of it," he said to Mo.

Mo nodded. "I'll get it to ya today."

"Go now," Claude ordered. "There ain't nothin' here that needs yer attention."

Mo's face fell. His shoulders slumped. He stood slowly, but obediently. "Yes, sir."

Without another look about, Mo was through the door and gone. Seeing the look of dejection on his face saddened me.

Claude didn't seem to notice that he'd crushed his son. He grumbled at me next. "Anythin' else?"

I was stunned to be right at the focus of his attentions.

"Er, no—" I stammered and backed from the kitchen. With no place to sit myself I grabbed my shawl and stepped onto the front porch. The morning was warming and the air grew heavy. The rain of the past few days added to the humidity that hung in the air. The day would be hot and miserable. The misery not only from the weather, but also from the fact that I'd have no bed to sleep in and no privacy. It seemed Joseph was to be my ward for the next few weeks, or until he was mended enough to be of use to Claude Moret again. I consoled myself with the knowledge that, so long as a valued member of the Moret gang was under my care, I'd be able to parlay that into medical supplies. And, as long as Joseph was under my roof, I might be able to glean some information about Finn from him.

Heavy boots fell as Claude and Jack Moret left the kitchen and walked through the front room. I stood and went to the door.

"Wake up!" Claude growled as he kicked at the other two men.

They both startled awake and jumped to their feet.

"Get the boats," Claude ordered.

The two brushed past me. Jack eyed me as I stood in the doorway, a smile playing at the corner of his mouth.

I realized I was still in my nightgown, and with the sun behind me, there was no telling what he could see. I pulled the shawl around my torso, trying to preserve some modesty. I quickly remembered my role with Jack, and I allowed a manufactured blush to warm my cheeks as I looked to the floor in a shamed manner.

Claude stomped in front of me and stopped. He stood tall, towering above me. I chanced a glance up at him. For all the hours he'd been in my house, I'd hardly gotten a good look at him. It felt dangerous to lay eyes upon the legend that was Claude Moret. It felt almost as if I was looking the devil himself directly in the eye.

Claude's skin was tanned and leathered. The furrowed lines of age and trouble wrinkled his brows and nearly engulfed his eyes. His light brown hair was dusted with grey as was the stubbly growth on his face. Despite his aged appearance, Claude's eyes were sharp. It was obvious that he was acutely aware of everything in front of him, and I imagined, of everything that brewed just below the surface.

Claude's frame was large and his chest obviously muscled. He was thicker than Mo, but he hadn't sacrificed his other physical attributes to age. It was easy to imagine Mo would look like this in thirty years. Only without the hard edge of danger.

"You'll get your supplies," he said. "But, he'd better not die."

I gulped. Suddenly I was uncertain of my assessment of Joseph's condition. What if a branch of the mesenteric arteries or the colon had been nicked? Joseph would certainly die a slow and painful death.

Claude didn't wait for a response. He stepped past me, moving from the porch toward the dock.

My eyes remained glued to him as he crossed the dock and stepped into the boat.

"Don't be scared, chér." Jack's breath was hot on my ear and drifted across my neck and shoulder. He leaned against me slightly, as he whispered in my ear. "I won't let him hurt you. You jus' be a good girl and do what needs done."

I fought off the repulsion that threatened to engulf my body.

Jack's lips lingering at the top of my ear, brushing ever so slightly. "I've missed you."

The shudder that rushed the length of my spine was difficult to control. I turned to face him, a flirty smile on my lips. "I'm sure you've got important business to occupy yourself with, Jack. Don't you tease me with yer flattery."

He drifted closer, and each time he leaned into me, I feared this would be the time I'd be unable to distract him. Unable to turn him away. The time would soon come that I'd be unable to put him off and he'd try to kiss me. "You'd better get along. I'm sure yer brother won't wait patiently for long."

A low growl emitted from Jack's throat. "I swear yer teasin' me. You know you drivin' me crazy, right?"

"I'm sure ye don't think I'd tease a man." I batted my eyes and jerked my jaw in the direction of the dock. "He's lookin' for ye."

Claude wasn't, but Jack was a good soldier and turned right away, trotting after his brother.

Tension poured from my body as they all pushed away from the docks. The two boats bobbed along on the waves until they disappeared around the bend. I watched until they were gone even though I was certain neither of them would look back toward me. And they didn't.

SEVEN

My kitchen was filled with children when Mo returned with the bandages and moonshine I'd requested.

I'd pulled the curtain closed that separated the kitchen from the front room so that nobody could see Joseph. It'd do no good for anyone to be talkin' about the man in my bed or the fact that he was a member of the Moret gang. I wasn't sure who'd stabbed Joseph, or even if anyone was looking for him, so I thought it best to avoid any outside attention.

"What's goin' on here?" Mo asked as he came in through the kitchen door.

In addition to the number of children gathered in the kitchen, there were at least six others waiting on the back porch.

"Ringworm," I said and laughed as Mo immediately jumped out of reach of the children.

The little girl on the chair in front of me squirmed as I pressed a rag with cider vinegar against the red raised welt on her elbow. I gave her mum the same instructions I'd repeated to the others. "Clean it with the vinegar every few hours. Have her wear sleeves to keep it covered when she's playing with other children. And be sure to clean the house from top to bottom."

She nodded as she ushered the little girl onto the porch and down the path.

My little fungal-infested patients left as they'd arrived: in one giggling, barely managed herd.

I dropped all the vinegar dampened rags into one large basin. "I'll have to boil the lot of them," I mumbled, more to myself than to Mo who still stood, pressed against the wall. "Oh, fer heaven's sake. Take a seat."

Mo regarded the chair where my last patient had been seated and the table around which the other children had gathered. He maintained a wide berth as he crossed the small room and placed the box of supplies on the counter. "There's all the bandages I could find. There's also two pints of shine. That should be enough. At least for a while. Don't let nobody see it, someone's likely to steal it."

I nodded. I was certain I had a small empty bottle I could pour it into that'd attract less attention. "Thank you."

"How's Joseph doin'?" His voice was low, hushed.

"Sleeping mostly. He's been having some pain, but that's to be expected. Yer free to talk to him if ye want."

He shook his head. "Nah. We ain't exactly friends. He's one of Jack's boys."

My ears pricked at this bit of information. Were there cracks in the Moret gang?

I busied myself with the soap and a rag, cleaning the sink and table area. My mind churned, trying to think of the best manner of getting more information from Mo. I matched his hushed tone with my own. "I assumed ye'r all together."

Mo walked over the doorway and pulled the curtain aside.

Through the opening I could see the heavy rise and fall of

Joseph's chest. He was deep in sleep, having had another few bumps of moonshine not even an hour before.

Mo turned back toward me. The curtain fell into place. Mo took a seat at the freshly cleaned table. "My uncle has his own fellas. They work directly for him."

I sat next to Mo. "I thought everyone worked for yer da?"

He nodded. "Technically they do. But when he ain't around they answer to Jack."

There was a subtle, but bitter tint in his voice as he said that.

I decided to try and push the issue. I stood and bustled about the kitchen as I talked, keeping an indirect eye on Mo the entire time though. "I guess I'd assumed that they'd answer to you when yer dad's not around."

"That's the way it was s'posed to be. Until recently."

"Oh? Did somethin' happen then?" I slid a glass of sweet tea in front of him then turned my attention to straightening the shelves.

"Nah," he sipped from his glass. His voice had the quality of someone lost in a memory. "Just differin' opinions."

A moan sounded from the front room.

Mo looked over his shoulder toward the doorway. He took another drink of his tea and stood. "I've got business. Let someone know if ya need any more supplies. My pére expects Joseph to be back to work. You make sure that happens."

He walked through the back door, leaving me standing in shock at the way he'd spoken to me. *Who the bloody hell, did Mo Moret think he was?*

"Girl!" Joseph's voice was gravelly as he called from the front room.

I looked from the hanging curtain that divided the rooms to the back door. Had Mo talked like that for Joseph's benefit?

"Do ya want me ta piss the bed or are ya gonna help me?"

Christ! It was going to be a long few weeks with Joseph. I became determined to get him healed and sent back to his boss in record time.

I pushed past the curtain. "Injured or not, if ye piss the bed ye'll lie in it, ye understand me?"

He startled as I shoved a bottle in his direction. "Ye'll piss in this until ye can get out of the bed."

Joseph recovered from his surprise quickly. A devious smile crept across his face. "Ain't ya gonna hold it for me?"

"I'll not be holdin' nothin' fer the likes of you. And you'll mind yerself while yer in my house. Do ye understand me?"

He leered at me. "Ya mean while I'm in Jack Moret's house."

I spun on him, not caring what he thought if me, wanting only to shut him up. "That's right. It's Jack's house. And I'm livin' here at *his* invitation." I stepped closer, towering over him and dropping my voice, leaning directly in front of his face. With my voice low, silky and full of implication I added, "How do ye think Jack would react if his *special* guest were badgered by ye? I don't think he'd take it well meself."

I stood straight and walked from the room. Over my shoulder I added, "Now take yer piss, and I'll get you somethin' to eat."

Joseph was on his best behavior the rest of the day. He answered every question with "Yes'm" and "no, Ma'am".

It was worth it to have him thinking I was Jack's lover to buy myself some degree of respect and freedom from his leering.

Joseph relied heavily on the moonshine for management of his pain, though I suspected he simply liked having a reason to imbibe.

As my bed was occupied, I pulled the armchair to the far wall and tucked myself into a ball under a blanket and tried to sleep.

In the middle of the night, I thought I heard a noise in the kitchen. I strained to hear anything in the other room before I rationalized that the sound I'd heard was probably just Joseph rolling over. Exhaustion took over and I slipped back into sleep.

The early morning light pulled me from my slumber. I unrolled from the chair, joints and muscles stiff from sleeping in the cramped chair. As I slowly rose from my sleeping position I looked at my patient. He slept facing the wall, breaths deep and even.

I stretched as I walked to the kitchen, letting the curtain fall behind me to muffle my sounds. I was in no mood to wake Joseph. It had been days since I'd had any time alone and I craved even a few moments of privacy.

On the table was a small sack. It hadn't been there when I'd gone to sleep. The noise I'd heard last night hadn't been my imagination, or Joseph moving after all. Someone had been in my kitchen.

The sack was secured with twine, which had been tied around several iris stalks. The brilliant purple-blue color of the blooms were beautiful, and I realized how long it had been since I'd had something so simple yet uplifting in my day-to-day life. I immediately trimmed the stalks and put the flowers into a jelly jar.

Inside the sack were stalks of asparagus, some carrots, cabbage, garlic, a few tangerines and several bright red, plump strawberries. I rinsed them all and left them on a towel to dry. Visions of an aromatic soup, simmering on the stove all day, filled my head.

I smiled as I chopped the vegetables and added fresh herbs to a simmering pot, imagining my benefactor sneaking in during the dark of night and leaving this gift on the table. I had no doubt it was Mo who'd left the goods.

"Smells good, ma'am." Joseph hobbled into the kitchen, bracing himself against the wall as he walked.

Ma'am? I knew I'd made some progress in demanding he show some respect but continuously calling me ma'am was quite a bit more of a progression than I'd imagined.

"It should be ready for supper. And not a minute before." I wouldn't have him trying to eat it before it was ready.

He eased himself gingerly into a chair at the table.

"Give me a minute and I'll put some coffee on." I cooked him two eggs and cut some of the berries and put them on a plate before him with the promised cup of coffee.

"Ye need to eat. Get yer strength up. I'm sure Claude is anxious fer ye to get back to work.

Joseph ate his breakfast as though he hadn't had a meal in a week. He even used a stale biscuit to mop up the remnants of egg and berry juice.

I picked at a biscuit as I determined how to dig for more information about the Morets. "What sort of work do ye do, anyway? Am I getting' ye healed up fer heavy liftin' or are ye more likely to be tellin' others what to lift?'

Joseph leaned back, hands trailing across his swollen belly. His eyes were direct and focused as he answered. "I do whatever's needed."

His response, so measured and rehearsed, unnerved me. He seemed to be daring me to ask more, while simultaneously warning me against doing so. I scrambled for a response that would make my question more innocent. "Well, if ye go liftin' anything heavy, ye'll tear the soft tissue open again. Best stick to tellin' others what to do."

Joseph considered my warning before pointing to the counter expectantly. "How 'bout one of those tangerines Jack brought? Can I have one?"

"Jack?"

He nodded. "Yeah. I seen him in the middle of the night. He left it all there. Stood in the doorway lookin' at us both fer a while before he left. I figure'd you'd seen him."

"No." The fact that Jack had been in the house without my knowledge was far more troubling than had it been Mo who'd left the surprise bounty. I grabbed a tangerine for Joseph. Suddenly, my appetite for soup wasn't nearly as strong.

Joseph and I spent a quiet morning. I helped him out to the porch after breakfast, so he could relax and look over the lake.

"I'm expecting people might start comin' by. Is there anything ye need?"

"There's a book on the table," he said. "Can I read that?"

I was surprised. I'd nearly forgotten about the book one of the boys left behind after being treated. Joseph didn't strike me as a reader. I retrieved the book from the small table next to my armchair.

"The Tower Treasure," he read the title.

"What's it about?"

He looked up at me. "Well, I don't know. Yet. But it has a treasure."

I smiled at his excitement of the treasure that might await him between the pages. He was firmly absorbed in his reading before I stepped back into the cabin and shut the door behind me.

I hurried into the kitchen and checked the back porch. Nobody was waiting for me yet.

With a big pot set in the sink and filled with vinegar and water. I stripped the blood-stained sheets from the bed and submerged them in the liquid to soak. I quickly replaced the soiled sheets with the one other set that had been left in the wardrobe. They were far more worn, but at least they were clean.

Odi was the first to arrive at my door. "I have a tummy ache," she complained.

I had no doubt that her love of sweets was partially to blame. I pulled peppermint leaves from the shelf and boiled them in a tea.

Moments after finishing her drink she exclaimed that she was cured and ran off—candy in hand—to continue her day.

I scrubbed the sheets as I waited for other patients. A faint pink stain remained, though you'd have to have known it was there to really notice.

Nobody else came to the door, so I closed it and went to check on Joseph.

"You ever been to New York?" he asked, looking up from his book.

"No."

He held the book up, finger firmly marking his place, and shook it in my direction. "Now, it ain't that I suspect you, but forty thousand dollars were stolen from the Tower Mansion and the thief definitely had red hair."

I rolled my eyes and shook my head.

Joseph laughed and returned to his reading.

I retrieved the sheets and carried them to the laundry line. On the east side of the cabin, the line was placed perfectly for exposure to the greatest hours of sunshine. I guessed they'd be completely dry in only a few hours.

By late afternoon I couldn't take Joseph's questioning any longer and finally let him have a bowl of soup. He actually had three before he leaned back and rubbed his belly. He winced then.

"Is it hurtin'?"

He nodded, his eyes pinched and brows pulled together.

"Ye did too much today," I chastised him. I retrieved the

moonshine and a glass and administered a hefty pour. I helped him back to the bed.

"One more swallow?"

I brought the cup with another hefty pour. I'd manage two goals: I'd ease Joseph's pain and give myself a few hours of privacy.

He was asleep before I'd rinsed his bowl. I looked about the kitchen and the irises caught my attention. Flowers left by Jack. I was disgusted and angry. *What the hell am I doing?*

I'd made no progress in finding out what happened to Finn. The only thing I'd accomplished is being tucked away by Jack Moret like some illicit lover while tending to the people who kept him safe. It wasn't only Joseph and the other gang members who protected Claude and Jack Moret. It was every person in Cleric's Cove. They all knew exactly who and what the Morets were about and turned a blind eye to their actions. It was the old people with their arthritic joints, the pregnant women, and the mothers with their fungus-infected, injury prone children. It was Leonie as well as Odi. Every one of them who came to my door and accepted my services while protecting the man who'd taken my brother from me.

I was just as bad. Because I'd softened my heart to these people. I'd treated them, listened to them, encouraged them. I'd even saved the life of one of Claude Moret's henchmen. I could have easily let him die, could have even hastened his death. But I'd chosen to save him so that they could go about their horrible business of making people disappear. So they could steal people from their families in the dark of the night.

I ripped the flowers from the jar and carried them through the house. I stalked out to the dock and flung them into the lake. I let out an animalistic yell as they hit the water and were swept away in the tide.

"Remind *me* not to bring you flowers," Mo's voice was hushed behind me.

I spun around. My anger firmly leading me, though I did manage to not yell at him. "*What* are you doin' here?"

"I just came ta check on ya. And bring ya this." Mo approached me as if approaching a rabid animal. His movements were slow and hesitant. His eyes wide, showing that he meant no threat. He held his hands out, offering something, though because of the dark, I couldn't tell what.

"What is it?"

"A bed roll. It ain't much, but it's got to be more comfortable than that chair."

How did he know? If it had been Jack in my kitchen last night, how did Mo know I was sleeping in the chair?

I stepped toward him and accepted the roll. "Thank you," I whispered.

I feared Joseph might wake and find Mo here. Certainly, he'd report that to Jack. There's no way I'd have been tasked with caring for him if he wasn't a loyal member of the gang. He'd keep none of my secrets.

Mo backed away. "I have to go. I just wanted to be sure you had that."

The dark engulfed him before I had the chance to say another word.

I carried the bedroll into the cabin and closed the door behind me. Before I put out the lamp in the front room I retrieved my knife from the wardrobe. I stepped into the kitchen and pulled the curtain behind me before strapping the blade to my thigh. There was no way I was going to be caught off guard by Jack in the middle of the night. I pushed aside the chairs and laid out the bedroll next to the wall. The pad wasn't terribly thick; it felt as though several layers of wool had been sewn together. It was better than the hard floor and far better than sleeping in that chair again. I retrieved the extra blanket from the armchair, blew out the candle, and lay down.

A soft bump near the window drew my attention. My right hand wrapped around the knife handle and I stilled, watching for movement. After several minutes I eased back onto the bedroll. I couldn't see anything through the window. I thought of Mo as I lay there. *He's one of them*, I reminded myself. *Just like everyone else, his sole purpose is protecting Claude Moret. And just like everyone else, he isn't to be trusted.*

But unlike everyone else, it was Mo that lingered in my dreams and warmed the parts of my heart that had grown cold with vengeance.

EIGHT

APRIL 17, 1930

It was three days before I saw another member of the Moret gang. And then, in the dark of night, they seemed to all show up within hours of each other.

Joseph and I had been sitting at the kitchen table playing cards when the door was flung open and a man rushed in. He held up his hands in front of him and made a "Ssh" motion with his mouth.

I was startled, but Joseph reached for me. He gripped my arm and gave me a silent reassurance when I looked at him. It was then I recognized the man as one of those who'd carried Joseph into the cabin that night. The one who nearly fainted at the sight of blood.

"Ya need to cover the windows," he commanded. "Everyone's commin'."

Everyone? What the hell could he mean by everyone?

I found a hammer and nails in the old shed out back. We nailed blankets over the window in both rooms.

Other men began to trickle in, each with a potato sack over their shoulder. Their wide eyes darted about the cabin, searching for some unknown threat. Every unexpected bump caused them to jump and twitch. They unloaded their bags. An assortment of coffee, metal dishware, and canned foods covered the counter. The men also had wool blankets rolled in the bottom of their packs.

I looked at Joseph, only slightly understanding that something had gone wrong. "What are they carrying?"

"Road bags," he said. "Everyone has one ready in case they have to hit the road fast."

Something had happened. My mind turned immediately to Mo. Had he been arrested? Had he been killed?

Saves me the trouble, I tried to rationalize with my impulses.

Men slipped into the cabin at intervals. There were twelve men when the last arrived. They nodded at each other but said little. The way they looked around, it was apparent that none of them knew what had gone wrong. They had simply gotten word and followed the established plan.

I started coffee and began to cook. If I was making biscuits, it wouldn't be so apparent that I was listening to their chit chat. I'd made two batches of biscuits and several pots of coffee before Mo stepped through the door. His eyes found mine before he glanced about the room to see who was present. When he saw that nobody was paying him much attention, he offered me a slight nod.

Relief loosened the grip on my chest. He was safe. It was both good news and bad. If Mo was alive and a free man, I might still have to take vengeance on him one day soon.

"What happened, Mo?" Joseph tried to stand, leaning against the table as he did so.

"The revenuers got Claude. He's in jail."

I turned my attention toward my mixing bowl as a bitter smile curled the corner of my mouth. Claude was in jail. It wasn't enough, not yet, but knowing that he wasn't running about Louisiana as a free man lifted my dark and vengeful spirits.

Behind me, the room filled with sounds of surprise and mumbling as the men communicated their disbelief to each other.

"What about Jack?" someone asked. "He should be here."

Mo's response was quick and bitter. "He should be. But he ran off like a scared mouse before my dad was even caught."

"So, he's free. He's in charge."

Mo spun on the man. His voice was full of fury as he towered over the older man. "He abandoned Claude before he was even caught. Left him to be arrested. He's a coward!"

The room grew quiet. I looked over my shoulder. Each man had his eyes fixed on the floor. None were willing to curse Jack for being a coward in case he came back to claim his charge, but they were also unwilling to deny Mo's claim in case he assumed the role.

"I'll bet it was them damn Grangers tipped off the rev'nuers," someone mumbled.

The others joined in agreement, and the conversation grew in the kitchen.

Mo looked at me. His eyes were dulled and seeking.

I tipped my head and gave him a sympathetic smile. I wanted him to know I was sorry for him, but that was something I couldn't say out loud, and not just because of the other people in the room.

Once I'd ensured everyone had coffee and biscuits, I grabbed my shawl. "I'm sure ye 'ave some discussing to do. I'll be sittin' out by the lake."

Mo nodded as I walked from the room.

I felt the burn of every man's eyes as I walked from the room.

"Have some respect," Mo growled as I pulled the door closed behind me.

The sounds of the lake and the chorus of nightlife surrounded me as I rocked.

I was lost in my thoughts. I was happy that Claude was in jail. I hoped he would be there for a long time. Although I had vowed to get revenge on Finn's behalf, I'd always feared the moment when I'd come face-to-face with him. The minute I'd have to make the decision that would forever cast me into his world. If I killed Claude, I'd be no better than him. But I was prepared to do it. I'd do it for Finn, and for Dad and Mum. But I knew I wouldn't emerge from the act unchanged. The pressure of the blade against my thigh was a reminder that one day my soul would be no less tarnished than a Moret's.

That would be the moment everything I ever was or hoped to be would die. Was I really prepared to walk through the flames of hell to avenge Finn, or was I fooling myself to think I was capable of embracing vengeance so easily?

The door opened quietly, and Mo stepped through. "We're done."

I nodded and looked back toward the lake. The moonlight caught the waves as they crested gently against each other and then folded. "I was just enjoying the night. Have ye ever felt like this moment, the one yer in right now, is the last time you'll be the same person? Like everything changes the minute it passes?"

Mo leaned against the porch railing. He'd left the door open and was directly across from it. It would be apparent to anyone in the cabin that, although Mo was talking to me, there was nothing secret or nefarious going on between us. Nothing to tell Jack about.

"I might be havin' one of those moments right now," he

said. His voice was low. There was no threat that it'd carry inside and be overheard.

"I'm sorry about yer dad," I said.

He crossed his arms and nodded. "Yeah. Well, it's a risk we know exists. Ya can only avoid it fer so long, I guess."

I yawned and pulled my shawl tighter around myself.

"Yer tired."

"I'm fine." Another yawn fought its way from my body. "Maybe a bit," I conceded.

"We could prob'ly all use some rest." He reached his hand toward me, beckoning me to come with him.

When I walked past Mo and through the door, I felt the warmth of his hand on my lower back as he guided me into the front room. It was only a moment, but it was hot, electrifying, and intense like the hand of Helios had been laid across my back.

Joseph had already self-administered his liquor and was nearly asleep on the bed already. From the looks of several of the other men, he'd been generous enough to share his tincture.

"Sam, you take first watch," Mo ordered. The man jumped up and was out the door without question. "Junior, Davey, Tim. You'll be taking the rest of the night. Two-hour shifts. You signal if you see hints of revenuers, or *anyone*."

They all nodded, and the ones who remained in the house began to lay out their bedrolls in the front room.

In the kitchen, I lowered myself onto my bedroll, glad to have my space already claimed. A few men had wandered into the kitchen, laying out their blankets while trying to maintain a respectful distance.

I'm about to sleep in a house with fourteen men, I thought. *Mum would be beside herself te see this.*

I studied the ceiling, imagining the heavens above. I wondered if she were indeed looking down on me. *Sorry, Mum.*

"This spot taken?" Mo held his own bedroll and indicated the space along the wall by my own.

"Help yerself," I said.

Someone turned down the lamp to a low flame. With the windows covered, no moonlight could penetrate the room. The flame of the lamp did little to illuminate the room. I could barely make out Mo's figure as he laid out his bedding.

The small blanket I'd rolled into a pillow was at the end that faced Mo. I turned on my side, one arm tucked under the pillow and helping support my head. With my arm bent, my knuckles brushed against the wall. I usually straightened my arm, but with Mo so close, I wasn't able to.

I listened to the sounds of breathing around me. The breaths deepened as the men fell into sleep. Some snored softly, others grunted periodically.

"I'm sorry about this," Mo whispered.

My stomach fluttered as if it sensed Mo's proximity and been waiting for some word from him. "About what?" I whispered back.

"For Joseph. For everyone bein' here." He paused for two beats before adding, "For Jack."

I lifted myself onto my forearms and pulled closer toward him so that I could drop my voice further. "I'm not with Jack. I never 'ave been." It felt important to me that he know that. For there to be no doubt in Mo's mind that I didn't have a relationship with his uncle.

"I know. But you have to know that he thinks you're his. He's told everyone you are. And that's dangerous. For you."

Fear fluttered through my body and churned in my stomach. Jack Moret had claimed me. That alone was a danger, but if Jack suspected that anyone was challenging his claim to me, that person—as well as myself—would be in grave danger.

"I won't let anything happen to you, Deary," Mo whispered.

My heart skipped. *He called me Deary.* The kids in Cleric's Cove had started calling me Deary, even some of their parents. Had Mo been asking about me? Had he simply been paying attention to what the people said about me?

I lowered my head and drifted to sleep with that question in my mind.

NINE

APRIL 18, 1930

I woke early.

The heavy blankets covering the windows kept the encroaching sunlight at bay.

I felt a weight and heat in my hand and twitched to shake it, imagining I'd slept on my arm wrong, and my hand had fallen asleep. The sensation wasn't numbness, but another person's hand.

I relaxed into the warmth of Mo's soft grasp. My fingertips brushed against the raised scar of his right palm. I closed my eyes and relished the feeling of Mo's hand around mine. I realized it had been months since I'd had any sort of intentional human contact. I hadn't held anyone's hand since the night Mum passed away. I'd detached and maintained a distance—physical and emotional— from everyone I'd come across since that night. Lying here, in the dark, I allowed myself a few moments to revel in having a connection with another person.

He's not like the others, my heart whispered.

He's a Moret. That makes him exactly *like the others*, my mind retorted.

65

I slipped my hand from Mo's, albeit slowly and while memorizing every detail about how it felt to be touched by him.

I tip toed from the kitchen. A man sat on the porch. *Tim?* He leapt from his perch and threw his cigarette away as I pulled the door behind me.

"I'm going into Cleric's Cove for some eggs," I said.

He nodded and returned to his chair.

I hurried along the path and knocked when I got to Leonie's place. I hoped Odi would be sleeping. I had no need for a curious child to see me getting such a large number of eggs.

Leonie opened the door. The smell of bacon and fresh bread wafted through the door around her.

"I'm sorry te bother ye so early, but I'm in need of some eggs."

She nodded and whispered, "Gimme a minute."

When she came out she had a basket. I followed her to the fenced yard, the chickens squawked and scurried as Leonie pushed through the gate.

"I've got some baking to do. I might need several," I said.

She nodded as she ducked into the coop. When she returned the basket was full to the brim. She'd packed some straw around them to protect them. "There's three dozen, "she said. "I imagine that'll take care of yer, uh, *baking* needs?"

I hadn't fooled her a bit. She—and probably everyone else in Cleric's Cove—knew that the Moret gang was in my cabin. *Jack Moret's cabin*, I corrected myself.

"Thank you. I'll repay you," I promised.

She shook her head. "No need to. It was the Morets that bought the chickens to begin with. The eggs are bought and paid for."

"Is there anything in Cleric's Cove that *isn't* bought and paid for by the Morets?" The words slipped out on their own and hung in the air between us.

Leonie glanced about as she latched the coop, gripped my elbow, and propelled me across the clearing. Her gaze was locked forward and voice low. "No. There's nothing, and *nobody*, here that the Morets don't own. And, you'd be well advised to stop asking questions. Ain't nobody 'round here gonna give up the Morets. You just go back and play yer part."

She gave me a soft shove and offered an exaggerated wave before turning back toward her house.

I returned to the cabin with a slightly broader under-standing of how fully ingrained Claude Moret was in this small haven. It was his. The whole place. There might even be other small communities along Lake Salvador who were also indebted to the Morets.

Several men crowded onto the porch, the bitter smell of their cigarettes hanging low under the awning. "Mornin', ma'am,"

I pulled the blanket covering the kitchen window back, then took out the skillet and lard and began to cook the eggs. There were plenty of biscuits left from the previous night for each man to have one more with his eggs.

As the smell of coffee and eggs drifted throughout the cabin, the still-sleeping men began to stir. They yawned and stretched. Several made other unpleasant noises as they woke.

I focused on the cooking. It was no easy feat to fry up three dozen eggs. Not to mention the endless pots of coffee they consumed. Each man brought his metal camp ware to collect his eggs. The men left with no more than a grunt of apprecia-tion. Some carried their plates onto the porch to eat, others sat on the floor. The sound of men slurping eggs and coffee echoed from the walls.

"Mornin'," Mo mumbled as he came beside me. He looked out the window as if that was his sole purpose for being so near me. *Was it? Was I simply imagining that Mo would find any other reason to be so near me?*

"Mornin'," I answered softly. My cheeks warmed, and I was certain it wasn't from the heat of the stove.

I handed him his plate.

"Thank you," he said. He lingered for several seconds, very near me, before he took his plate to the table.

A chair scraped as one of the other men hastened to rise and offer Mo his seat. "Here, Boss," a gravelly voice said.

Mo accepted the seat with no acknowledgment of the man who'd given it up.

I started cleaning the breakfast mess.

"Junior?" I wasn't sure which one he was, I only remembered that Mo had referred to him last night.

"Yeah?" a voice called from the porch.

"Take the bucket to the well and get water." I handed him the bucket and turned before he could object. "You'll probably need to make two trips. There's a lot of clean up to do," I called over my shoulder as I walked back into the kitchen.

Joseph carried his own plate into the kitchen as Junior arrived with the first bucket. He set it on the counter, and as he turned, I caught Mo pointing at Joseph and his dish. Joseph turned around and immediately began to wash down his dish in the basin I'd poured.

Each of the men followed suite, washing their own dishes. I tried to not show my appall as many of them walked away, drying their dish on the hem of their dirty shirts. *At least they're not expecting me to clean up after them.*

They gathered in the living room to talk after eating. I busied myself cleaning up the counters and skillet while keeping an ear keenly tuned toward the front room.

"We got a delivery to make tonight," Mo said. "Even if Claude ain't here to make it, we have to. It's fifteen gallons, but this buyer'll open us up to Metairie and all them people buildin' them big houses up at Metairie Road."

"I'll get a message to the buyer. We'll change the drop. Nobody'll be lookin' fer us near the old Bayton farmhouse."

Mo shook his head. "That's gettin' awful close to Point de Concession. We can't have the Grangers thinkin' we're moving in on their territory. We got enough trouble."

"We'll go south then. I'll find a place."

Mo nodded. "Get a message out right away. You know the score. We ain't got much time."

Three of the men left. They paused in the kitchen long enough to pack their bedrolls and dishes into their bags before they walked out of the cabin and into the trees.

I assumed we wouldn't be seeing them again any time soon.

Mo continued talking. "Everyone else get back to work. Keep your eyes out for trouble. Have one man posted at all times. We can't afford to lose a single still or miss a run."

The men began to roll their own bedding and pack it into their sacks.

"And if ye get busted, nobody says a word. You're with us until you ain't. And if you make that decision, it's final, no comin' back." Mo's words were heavy with unsaid meaning.

"There ain't no cause to worry, Mo." The man who spoke was old. His white hair may have been the darkest ebony at one time. "We're Moret. Forever."

Mo nodded as the men gathered their belongings and filed out through the back door.

A few nodded as they passed me. Others offered a simple "Ma'am," as they left.

It was as if the storm that settled into the cabin overnight was suddenly swept out to sea. A calmness descended over the small rooms. Silence settled once again into the corners.

"What about me, Mo?" Joseph asked. He'd pulled himself

up to the edge of the bed. One arm was wrapped around his abdomen, splinting his stomach from the pressure of movement and the pull of gravity.

Mo slumped in the armchair and rubbed his hands against his swollen eyes. "What about you, Joseph? You ain't in no condition to leave here."

"Sure, I can." His face pinched as he tried to scoot closer to the edge of the bed. He looked to me for confirmation. "Ain't that right?"

Mo and Joseph both looked at me. One with expectation coloring his face, the other with sad amusement.

I shook my head. Sorry to deny Joseph the opportunity to be of help. "No," I answered.

He leaned back in the bed and reached for the bottle of shine on the floor next to him. He took a long pull from it before lying down again. "Well then I may as well get good and drunk."

Shaking my head again, I turned to the kitchen. If Joseph was going to drink himself into a stupor, I was happy to let him do so. I made myself a glass of lemonade and left one on the counter in case Mo wanted one as well.

With my drink in hand, I escaped the warming interior of the house for the shaded back porch. The two original chairs had been joined by three others and a bench in the time I'd been staying here. Brought and left by my patients, I imagined. They'd rather leave their own chairs on my porch than be forced to stand while waiting for their turn to be seen.

I pulled the bench in front of the chairs so that I could put my feet up and stare out at the trees. I loved the way the Spanish moss danced from the branches. It flowed and billowed with the grace of a ballerina or an angel floating amongst the clouds.

The swaying of the leaves in the breeze caused sunlight to

sparkle through. Light danced along the base of the oak trees, making the ridges undulate as though the tree itself was a moving organism, responding to the warmth of the sun.

Birds called from the tree tops. The noises of animals that I still wasn't familiar with joined the sound of the surf and the constantly evolving natural music of Cleric's Cove.

The door opened, and Mo came out with the glass of lemonade I'd left for him. He sat on the bench, brushing against my feet as he did.

"What's that sound," I asked. "It's like a bugling sound. Is it a bird?"

He keened his ear toward the trees then smiled at me. "They're whooping cranes. Probably defending their territory."

"I've never heard anything like it. At least not until I came here."

Mo fidgeted. He took a deep breath and ran a hand through his curls. "Deirdre, I'm gonna have to stay here a while. I was with my dad when the rev'nuers showed up. One of them was shot."

I gasped and sat upright.

Mo laid a hand on my shin, then seemed to realize his mistaken impulse before pulling his hand away. "I didn't do it. But they're gonna be lookin' for me. I'm, uh, I'm in hiding, and I got nowhere else to go."

"Of course. It's yer family's place. It's where ye should be." My heart and mind clashed again. Mo would be staying here, with me—and with Joseph.

"I meant what I said last night," he said. "I won't let anythin' happen to you."

There were no words I could say that wouldn't betray me in one way or another.

Mo leaned closer. "I get the feeling that you're runnin' from something, Deirdre. I don't ever want you to think you have to run from me."

He stood and reached out, his fingers brushing along my jawline before he turned and returned to the dark interior of the cabin.

My chest burned with the breath that had become trapped in it. Emotion thundered in my chest. *Why? Why couldn't Mo be as awful as his father and his uncle?* It would be so much easier if I could hate him like any other Moret. But I didn't.

TEN

APRIL 19, 1930

The following afternoon I was returning from Cleric's Cove with supplies and food when I heard Mo yelling.

I ran along the path, growing more frightened with every passing second that I'd come around the corner to find Mo being hauled away by Prohibition agents.

Rounding the path, I saw that there was a boat tied to the dock. I hurriedly climbed the back porch, quietly opening the door and slipping through. I placed the supplies on the counter and crossed the room, pressing against the wall near the doorway to listen.

Voices were coming from the front room, only Mo's was raised.

"Who the hell was it?"

A sheepish voice followed. "Nobody knows, Mo. She said her name was Marline Fortune. Her driver was some guy she called Sonny. James's boys said he looked a lot like one of the Grangers though. Thought it might be the middle one. Ronny?"

There was a sliver of space between the curtain and the door jamb separating the kitchen and front room. I peeked through the space. Mo sat in the armchair with two men in front of him, holding their hats in their hands. Joseph laid on his side in the bed.

"Remy," Mo growled. "Remy Granger. Find out who that girl was. I want to know who's moving in on Moret business. We ain't gonna stand for this shit. I want to talk to James myself."

Granger. I'd heard the name mentioned several times already. I wondered who the Grangers were and what their relationship was with the Morets. It didn't sound like they were on a friendly basis. Maybe Finn had run afoul of the Grangers and not the Morets after all. Hope sprung in my chest and brought relief trailing behind it. If the Grangers had been the ones to hurt Finn, I wouldn't have to continue on my path to avenge him with the Morets. With Mo.

"You got it, Mo." One of the men stood, ready to leave.

His partner paused and dared one final question. "Any word on Jack?"

Mo leveled a cold look at the man. "If I get word about Jack, I'll let you know. When *you need to know.*"

"Right, Mo. Sorry. Was just curious was all." Both men rushed through the front door and made their way toward the dock without another word.

Mo went to the door and looked after them as the boat pulled away.

"They don't mean nothin'," Joseph said to Mo from the bed. "They're young and dumb. They don't get how to adapt to the situation. They only know what they was told to do if anything happened to Claude."

"Is that what you're doin', Joseph? Adapting?" Mo looked over his shoulder.

"Well, Mo, I ain't really got a choice, do I? I lost that when you stabbed me in the belly."

I slapped both hands across my mouth so as to not let a

gasp escape my lips. My eyes were so wide I could feel the pressure as they strained against the confines of their sockets.

"And the next time you pull a knife on me, I'll take it from you and stab you again. Only next time, I'll put a little more effort into gettin' it past yer fat gut."

Joseph struggled to sit up. I wasn't sure if it was because he wanted to look Mo in the eye or if he wanted to be in a better position to defend himself should Mo attack. "Come on, Mo. It was a disagreement. Yeah, Jack brought me in, but I'm loyal to the business. This ain't one man's game. We're a team and it takes all of us. Jack skipped out. You're runnin' things now."

"And when Jack comes back?"

"I don't know, Mo. It's gonna be a battle of the titans I'm afraid. Ain't neither of ya want to answer to the other."

I'd heard enough. I was overwhelmed with the amount of information I'd just learned. Mo and Jack were at odds. They both wanted to run the Moret empire. With Claude in jail, they might just bring each other down.

My mind reeled. If I could find a way to help ensure Mo destroyed Jack, I'd only have Claude to tend to myself.

My stomach turned with nervous energy. Not only had Mo stabbed Joseph, he had actually helped carry the man he'd stabbed in order to get him medical attention. Was Mo really so different from the rest of the Morets? Was he the sole redeeming member of an entire family?

I slipped out of the kitchen to the back porch and sat with my back to the wall. My hands clenched in my lap. *Mo stabbed Joseph.* That fact reverberated in my thoughts. Mo Moret was *not* an innocent. Had Finn come into conflict with him as well?

After several minutes, I regained my breath and my muscles loosened. I returned to the kitchen to put away the supplies and groceries I'd brought back with me.

Joseph shuffled into the kitchen, arm holding tightly to his abdomen. "Did ya get any more medicine?"

He'd taken to calling the whiskey his medicine.

I cast a glance into the front room. It was empty. Mo must have left through the front door.

I scoffed at Joseph. "It isn't the kind of thing I can just ask for."

"Sure, it is. Ev'ryone knows yer the Moret healer. You can have anything ya want. Ain't nobody gonna say no."

"And perhaps ye should lay off it a bit," I added before feeling immediately guilty for telling a man who'd been stabbed that he couldn't have a drop of liquor if that's what made him feel better.

"I'm sorry. I'll see about gettin' ye some more." I dug behind my jars of herbs and withdrew a jelly jar that I'd filled with moonshine. "Here. This should keep ye."

"Ya know you're a saint? I been tellin' Mo that you've been sent from the heavens." He took a long pull from the jar and shivered as the alcohol passed over his tongue and down his gullet.

"Of course, he don't believe me," Joseph laughed.

A dull ache burned through my chest at his words. Did Mo distrust me?

Joseph rolled to the side, the moonshine he'd been drinking throughout the day catching up to him. He laughed again and then looked to me with his most deliberate attempt at a serious face. His lids were at half-mast and one side of his mouth drooped. "I'm the only one who really appreciates you. The only one who knows what an angel you are."

I shook my head, realizing I'd been put on by a drunken fool.

"Git ta bed, ye drunkard." I hefted him to his feet and

ensured he made it safely to the bedroom without tearing the healing tissue at his abdomen.

I struggled to lift his feet into the bed then covered him with a sheet. It was barely six and hadn't cooled off entirely yet. The blankets still covered the windows, so I pulled the curtain to the kitchen closed behind me, leaving him in the mostly dark front room.

For the first time in what seemed like weeks, I had time alone. I pulled the mortar and pestle as well as a large knife from the shelves and arranged some dried herbs, flowers and plants on the table. Everything I'd learned about natural remedies and folk healing had been taught by Mam. Her own family was from a series of small sparse communities. Without an actual physician, they'd come to be relied on as village healers.

As I chopped and ground the leaves, roots and blossoms, then placed each in a small jar, I hummed an old Irish tune that Mam had taught me. It was the same tune that she'd worked to and had learned from her own mam. I was educated on a steady diet of information about herbal remedies. I was aware of which could heal a man, as well as which could end one. I foraged with my mum and learned which ingredients to dry, chop, and grind. Which could be taken orally, and which needed to be diluted, applied as a paste, or administered in a suspension.

My father was a physician. He was from a long line of Cassidy physicians. Though he'd trained in London and had been part of small practice in Dublin, he'd found his happiness when he returned to Finnigan's End and began working in and around the community he'd been raised in. It was from him that I learned the most about treating emergencies and delivering babies. I'd learned to set bones, dress wounds, sew lacerations, and deliver a breech baby in a manner that protected both the mum and babe.

The smell of elderberry leaves, lavender, peppermint and the soil-rich aroma of mallow and menguilié roots filled the kitchen when I'd finished. I wiped down the table and rinsed my hands. With a fresh cup of tea in hand, I opened the door to the back porch.

"Oh!" I tried to recover quickly and not show my surprise to find Mo sitting in the dark.

"Sorry," he said. "Been sittin' here a while. Just thinkin' 'bout things."

I held up my tea. "Can I get ye a cuppa?"

"Nah." He shook his head. He lifted a cigarette to his lips and pulled a matchstick from his pocket. With a flick of his wrist, he'd flipped it down and against the chair he sat on. A flame sprung to life and danced at the tips of his fingers. The orange glow billowed against the indigo night. The scent of sulfur mingled with the earthy aroma of my tea and the wafting remnants of the dried and pummeled medicinals. He cupped the flame in his hand as he took quick puffs, drawing the flame against the end of the cigarette.

I watched mesmerized. I was as entranced by the pull of the flame and gusts of smoke as I was with the way Mo's lips wrapped softly around the cigarette. A tremble erupted in my chest, my heart and lungs working as cohorts to prevent me from drawing a full breath. My own lips suddenly felt dry. I realized it might be because I'd pulled my lower lip between my teeth to prevent myself from licking them. I realized right away that either may be deemed a suggestive move should Mo see it.

Hurriedly, I lifted my cup to my mouth and sipped my tea. I nearly choked due to the tizzy I'd gotten myself into.

Mo patted the chair next to him. "Have a seat."

With my body revolting against me, I focused closely on my feet. I placed one in front of the other and then sat in the chair.

The last thing I needed was to trip and fall into his lap. I was certain I'd never live down that humility.

Why do you even care? My mind was screaming at me. *He's a Moret, and you're here for the sole purpose of finding and avenging Finn.*

Why was it that my heart and mind engaged in such intense battles every time Mo was around? I'd never forgotten my purpose around Jack. Or even in that brief time I'd spent in the presence of Claude Moret. But, with Mo...

He's different, my desperate and traitorous heart whispered again before I squelched its voice.

Mo took a deep drag from his cigarette and leaned back in the chair. He kicked one boot up on the bench across from us. He turned toward me slightly, elbow cast over the back of the chair. He leaned out of the smoke that lingered after he'd exhaled. It billowed softly about his head before it rose into the dark of the night like a ghost. "So, how much of that did ya hear earlier?"

I paused. I was afraid to admit that I'd overheard anything about his family business. His *criminal business.* I wasn't stupid enough to think that I wouldn't be deemed as a risk for everything I'd heard. But I was pulled by my own deeply ingrained ethical code. The one instilled in me by my parents. "If ye never lie, Deary, ye'll never 'ave to recall yer lies. Ye stick te the truth, and the truth'll stick right back to you," me dad used to say.

I let out a deep breath and turned to Mo. "Most of it, I think. I'm sorry 'bout yer—" I stumbled, unsure if I should even say the word "moonshine" out loud. "Yer stuff gettin' stolen."

"Yeah. Claude ain't gonna be happy. I been in charge three days and had fifteen gallons of shine stolen. But when I find out who stole our sale—"

He didn't have to finish the threat. It hung clear and heavy as the summer air in the bayou.

I tried to distract him from his thoughts of vengeance. "You've certainly stepped in to take care of everything. I'm sure yer dad will be proud of ye."

Mo snickered and shook his head. "Nah. Even if I hadn't gotten that stuff stolen, he'd have found somethin' I did wrong. That's the way Claude is."

An awkward silence descended around us. I sipped my tea while Mo focused his attention on his cigarette.

The one question that was ricocheting about in my brain was the one I didn't dare ask. "Why did you stab, Joseph?"

Apparently, I wasn't going to just dance around that question after all.

Mo blew the smoke from his lungs in a slow stream and tossed the cigarette to the soil path at the end of the porch. He leaned back but looked into the darkness rather than at me. "Joseph pulled a knife on me. I had to defend myself. When I got the knife from him, he shouted for someone to give him a gun. He was reachin' out, and I couldn't take the risk that some-one'd let him shoot me. So, I stabbed him."

My voice was low, nearly whispered. I couldn't force enough air from my lungs to give it any more weight. "There were other people there?"

He nodded.

"And they were watchin' him attack ye?"

Mo cast a quick glance at me as he nodded. "Yep."

"Who would do such a thing? Who would stand by as someone tried to stab ye?"

Mo leaned forward. He rubbed his fingers across his brow several times before he answered, "Jack. And Claude."

I gasped. "Yer own dad?"

I recalled the night they'd carried Joseph into the cabin. At the time I'd assume the quiet and somber mood of every man in the room had simply been because one of their members had been injured. Perhaps I imagined they were concerned about their friend. Now I realized how deplorable the events of that night had been. Mo's uncle and dad had been standing aside watching as Joseph tried to stab Mo.

Joseph—and even Mo—had expected that one of them might hand Joseph a gun to finish the job.

A curse slipped through my lips on the deep and bewildered sigh. "Holy Mother of Christ."

"That about sums it up," Mo responded.

It wasn't just the shock of what Mo had experienced that overwhelmed me. The fact that these men—the Morets—could so callously try to end a member of their own family meant that they would have even less regard for a life they hadn't created. It meant that—had Finn run afoul of the Morets—they would have easily dispatched him without a moment's hesitation.

The heavy weight of melancholy settled across my shoulders smothering the miniscule spark of optimism I'd carried with me into Moret territory. I wouldn't find Finn. I'd never see him again and I couldn't trick myself into holding out hope any more. My mind accepted what this pit in my stomach had known immediately: Finn was dead.

I blinked against the burn of tears that threatened to gather in my eyes. Grief and fear tumbled in my chest, drowning out any other feeling. *Finn is gone.* The only thing left for me was to destroy the Morets. Whoever had killed Finn—as well as whoever had ordered it, and anyone who stood by as he was robbed of his life—would pay. I might well die in the process, but I was prepared to meet my parents and Finn in the afterlife with the story of how I'd avenged everything that'd been stolen from us.

"Why?" It seemed that if I could better understand what Mo had done to cause his own dad to stand by as he was nearly killed, I'd better understand what kind of person Mo was.

"I made a mistake," he said. "A mistake I ain't never gonna make again."

I waited, but he said no more.

After a few minutes, he shook slightly, casting off unpleasant memories, or the serious mood that descended over us. He stood and held a hand out as if to help me up as well. "It's late. We should prob'ly turn in."

I reached up, my hand melting into his. As I stood, I felt his other hand against the small of my back, and he nodded for me to enter the kitchen first. I looked up as I moved past him. My shoulder brushed against the soft material of his shirt. His muscled chest rose and fell, each breath bringing the heat of his body closer to me.

Mo's face was so close to my own, and I gazed up at him. A spark of electricity jolted through my heart as Mo's eyes held mine. I imagined myself leaning into him, pressing my lips against his and being engulfed in his arms, the heat of his body pressed against mine. Desire coursed through my body, settling low in my belly as my breath hitched in my chest.

Mo leaned back as if he had seen each of my thoughts in vivid detail.

Embarrassment warmed my cheeks, and I hurried past him into the kitchen. I quickly rinsed my cup in the basin and set it on a towel.

As Mo reached the door, he stopped and looked out into the dark for several seconds.

I wondered if he'd heard something or was just being cautious.

"What is it?" I looked through the window since the blanket that had been hung over it was still pulled aside from earlier in the morning. I saw nothing but my own reflection peering back at me.

"Nothing." Shaking his head, he stepped in and closed the

door behind him. He moved a chair from the table and wedged it under the door knob.

When he turned, he must have seen the concern on my face. "Just a precaution."

He took another chair into the front room, and I heard the scraping of wood against wood as he secured the front door in the same manner.

My nerves were on edge at Mo's sudden concern for safety. The shadows cast by the oil lamp caused the night to take on a more sinister feel. I pulled the blanket back down over the window and laid down on my bedroll. Rolling my head from side to side, I tried to stretch out the tension that had settled into my shoulders from the days of uncertainty—and sleeping on the floor.

"Tomorrow I'll get Joseph out of your bed," Mo said. His voice was low so as to not wake up my slumbering—and snoring—patient.

I shook my head. "He's not healed yet. There's no way he could lift himself from the floor without tearing the new tissue. I'm fine where I am."

"Well, I'll move in there with him. You should have your privacy." Mo bent over and retrieved his own blanket and makeshift pillow before turning down the flame on the lamp.

The soft scratching of his boots against the planks of the floor as he left the kitchen and entered the front room echoed around me.

I wanted to call out to him. My mind came up with a dozen reasons why he should stay. *I'm scared. You were already there, no need to move. I don't like to be alone. I'm safer if you're close.* But the one that was most true: *I want to feel you near me.*

My ears strained at the sounds of Mo laying out his blanket in the next room. His boots thumped against the floor as he kicked them off.

I smiled as I heard the distinct sound of Mo picking the boots up and lining them neatly somewhere in his reach.

His clothing rustled against the blanket as he laid down and assumed a comfortable position.

The sound of his breaths didn't reach me. There wasn't the distinct sound of increased depth of respirations that would indicate he was sleeping.

I slowed my own breathing, listening more closely for Mo's.

Was he doing the same? I imagined Mo laying on his side listening for me.

I sent a silent plea to the universe and to Mo. *Please be innocent. Show me that yer not like yer dad. That yer nothin' like yer uncle. I know yer different. You have to be different.*

Because what did it say about me if I'd fallen in love with my brother's killer?

And if I had to kill Mo—and I would if he'd been the one to hurt Finn—I'd be no better a person than Claude or Jack Moret.

ELEVEN

The following two weeks were uneventful.

Mo managed the Moret business as men stopped by at all times of day and night to inform him of deliveries and bring money and supplies. I tried to maintain a respectful distance while he tended to his business. But I also strained to overhear anything I could use against his father.

I was gathering information on the Moret's bootlegging business as well as their other criminal endeavors: fencing of stolen property, blackmail of judges and police, there was even a brothel located in a very wealthy neighborhood in New Orleans. I was determined that, even if I couldn't kill Claude Moret, if he remained in jail, I'd have enough information to bring his entire enterprise crumbling down.

Joseph continued to heal. I rationed his liquor more vigilantly. He wasn't pleased to be denied, but soon found himself a purpose sitting outside. A shotgun—a gift that had been delivered along with groceries by members of the Moret gang— laid across his lap.

"I better not see that pointed at me," Mo growled at Joseph the first day he'd assumed guard duty.

"Well then, don't go givin' me a reason to," Joseph joked.

They'd settled into a friendly discourse, but periodically I caught sight of the defensive walls they'd erected between each other. Their distrust still lingered just below the foundation of the mutual interest they'd developed: their safety.

I ventured into Cleric's Cove every morning because, with Morets on the run and Mo in hiding at the cabin, the people wouldn't come to my door.

Each day, I tucked a few candies or pralines in my pocket for the children.

"Yer spoilin' that girl," Mo said as I walked past him one day. He'd been out on the boat fishing and was returning to the cabin with a bucket in one hand.

I peeked over the edge of the bucket and saw several fresh trout. "I don't know who yer talkin' about. And ye better be planning to clean those fish. Don't ye leave them fer me to do."

The devil's smiled slid into place on Mo's lips as I brushed past him.

"Tell Odi I said she'd best be listenin' to her mére. Leonie's got her hands full with that girl," Mo called after me.

There was little need for me in the village that day, so I joined Leonie under the shade of a tree, and we watched the kids play. I'd spent a lot of time with her and had even come to consider her a friend. I hoped to find a subtle way to ask her more about the Morets—and Mo in particular.

"You know you ain't got to come ev'ry day, right? If someone *really* needs help, someone'll come for ya."

"I just worry. I went from seeing several people every day to nobody coming to my door since—." I didn't dare continue. Even though I knew Leonie was well aware of who was likely hiding at the cabin, it seemed like a breach of trust to say the words. Also, since it was evident that Cleric's Cove had been bought and paid for by the Morets, I didn't want to risk word getting around that I was talking against them. It did me no good if the Morets distrusted me.

Leonie smiled and swatted at the bottom of a toddler that ran past her with an armful of leaves as if he was going to throw them at her. "You got nothin' to be concerned about. We're doin' our thing and you're doin' yours. We been without a doctor for a long time and we managed just fine. Besides, you wasn't brought here to tend to us."

The acidic rise of disgust burned in my belly as I realized that Leonie was referring to Jack and his claim on me. Jack's claim that I belonged to him.

"Of course, I was," I tried to detract from the rumor, to reassert the validity of my presence as a nurse. "I'm a trained nurse. Mr. Moret said Cleric's Cove was in need of a medic. *That's* why I'm here."

She laughed. "*Mr. Moret?* I'm sure it's convenient that you're a healer. That makes the story Jack tells his wife more believable than all the others."

Shame and fury lit through me. I shot from the chair suddenly, feeling the confines of the trap I'd allowed myself to be caught up in. Without another word to Leonie, I hurried along the path through the lush vegetation, desperate to be alone with my ire and humiliation.

As I approached the cabin, Mo looked up from where he cleaned the fish just off the back porch. I stomped onto the porch and threw open the kitchen door. Joseph sat at the table, hunkered over a bowl of something. His eyes were wide as I stormed into the room.

At the sight of him, I let out a carnal yell.

All I wanted was a moment alone, and at every turn I was met with the face of a Moret. Whether by blood or business, they were all Moret.

I stormed through the cabin, throwing open the front

door. I ran, bounding down the steps, to the water line and along the shore of the lake. Rocks crunched under my feet. The waves licked at my feet as they pounded along the soft soil.

My breaths grew raspy, and the air burned as my lungs drew each one in. The thundering of my heart echoed in my ears. My legs quavered, unaccustomed to the pace they kept and the unsteady terrain they fought against.

I drew a ragged breath through my nose, filling my burning lungs with more air and pushed on farther. It would be better to force myself to run the entirety of Lake Salvador than to let anyone see the tears of humiliation and frustration threatening to appear on a now daily basis. But I was determined to choke back those damned tears. There was no way I was going to let Claude Moret drive me into a weeping state.

I didn't make it around the lake though. Not even close.

Exhaustion gripped me as suddenly as my fury had spurred me on. I collapsed forward, hands on my knees as I drew ragged breaths. I struggled to gain control over my breathing, pulling fresh air deeply through my nose and pushing it back out through my mouth.

After several moments, I stood, lifting my arms over my head to open up my diaphragm as I'd seen coaches teach their athletes to do. My legs tingled, and heat flooded through them as the blood was carried to muscles I rarely challenged in my daily life.

It was several minutes before my ragged breaths grew even again.

I turned to survey the distance I'd have to travel back to the cabin, certain that a long walk faced me. The cabin, though small in the distance, was still easily visible. I'd run no more than a quarter mile I guessed.

"Fer feck's sake," I mumbled. It was what Mum used too

when she was frustrated. I kicked at the soil and began the short walk back.

I paused at the dock, looking out over the water for several minutes. I'd made a critical error in believing that Leonie might be my friend. She wasn't a friend of mine; she was simply part of the extensive buffer around the Morets. I'd been a fool.

Is this entire plan foolish? Can I ever really destroy Claude Moret or am I just fooling myself to think I could avenge my brother?

A shudder washed over me as I looked over the rolling waves. I glanced over my left shoulder, something drawing my attention to the thick vegetation behind me.

The tree line was thick and dark with the tangled weaving of trees and shrubs left to grow wild. Though I couldn't see anything, I had the distinct feeling that someone was undoubtedly looking back at me. I felt the burn of eyes scrutinizing my every move.

I turned my gaze back to the lake, while my attention was firmly focused on what lie behind me. My skin prickled, and my heart thrummed. I recognized the innate warning systems nature had planted deep in our most animalistic selves. I forced myself to walk slowly back toward the cabin. I even stopped to look out at the lake again and bent to picked up a feather that lay on the ground.

Mo was standing on the front porch, leaning against the door frame, when I reached it. "You alright?"

As I brushed past him into the house, I mumbled a warning. "There's someone in the bushes."

I paced in the front room as I waited for him.

Mo stood in the doorway for several more minutes, inspecting the surroundings from the corner of his eye as he pretended to be cleaning dirt from under his fingernails.

He finally came back into the house and closed the door behind him. Without a word to me, he went to the back door and gestured to Joseph, who was sitting guard on the back porch. Mo snapped to get Joseph's attention. With two fingers, he pointed to his own eyes and then in the direction of the tree line where I'd sensed the presence.

He closed the door quietly and reached his hand on top of the kitchen shelves. I was surprised when he withdrew a pistol and slid it into the waist of his pants at his back.

"Who is it?" I was both frustrated and grateful about the blankets that still hung in front of the windows. They prevented anyone from peering in at us, but also prevented me from being able to look out and see anyone who might approach the cabin.

Mo pushed the blanket aside a fraction of an inch and peaked out. "I don't know. Could be the law."

Or? I wanted to ask.

I sat at the edge of the armchair, ready to jump up and flee at the first sign the threat had grown more certain.

Mo remained at the window. He stood still, not betraying his caution with even the movement of his own breaths. It seemed impossible that a person could stand so motionless.

When he finally eased away from the window, Mo sat across from me at the edge of the bed. "Whoever it was, I don't think they're there anymore."

"But they might come back." I realized the risk to myself no matter who it was. If I was found in hiding with the Morets, I'd be guilty of collusion. But, if it was Jack—and I realized there was a real chance that he could be in hiding just outside my door—and he suspected Mo or Joseph had tried to move in on his "claim", I'd be in just as much, if not more, trouble.

"We have to be ready to leave. Fast," Mo said. He stood and rummaged through the shelves in the kitchen. He returned with a burlap sack that had been full of produce. "Put a few tins of food in it. Roll up your bedding every morning and put it in here. If there's anything you can't live without, it'd better fit in the bag, or you need to figure how to live without it."

I gathered a can of pears, one of tuna, and a can of beans and slipped them into the sack. I rolled a clean change of clothes and my shawl together and pushed them deep into the bag. With my bedroll, I wasn't certain I could possibly fit—or carry—another item.

Hours later, I remembered the one thing I couldn't bear to leave behind. I reached into the back corner of the wardrobe and under the cloche hat I'd relegated to the deep recesses of the cabinet. The chain was cool and light as my fingers pinched it and pulled it into my palm. I looked around the corner as I withdrew it. Mo was at the back door talking softly to Joseph.

I quickly slipped the chain around my neck, my thumb fumbling with the latch several times before I was able to get it hooked securely. I slipped the locket into neckline of my dress.

Darkness engulfed the cabin as the sun set. There hadn't been any other indications of anyone watching, but our nerves remained keenly attuned to any change or sense of danger. Joseph even abstained from his evening 'medicinals' after supper.

"I think I'll stay out on the back porch and keep an eye out tonight." He took the shotgun and used a light blanket to pad the chair before settling in.

"Can I get you anything?" I felt guilty, but much more comfortable, knowing that Joseph would be sitting watch through the night.

"Nah, I'll be fine. This ain't my first night shift."

When I returned to the front room, I found Mo slipping the clean bedding from the wardrobe onto the bed. "You may as well get a good night's sleep."

I smiled and stepped past the freshly made bed to pull the blanket back and steal a look through the window. "I don't see how that's possible. Every nerve in my body is jumping. Every time I hear a sound I'm certain someone is about to burst through the door."

Mo stepped behind me and took my wrist gently, causing me to let the blanket fall back across the window. His breath tickled my neck as he said, "I told ya I ain't gonna let anything happen to you."

I turned my head toward him, looking up into his eyes. Everything he said was in earnest. Mo believed he could protect me, he had no doubt that he'd do whatever it took.

His voice dropped to a whisper. "You have to trust me, Deirdre."

He looked intensely into my eyes as he stepped back and pulled me gently by my wrist.

Mo led me across the small room, his gaze never leaving my own. He stopped at the bed and pulled me closer, his free hand slipping to my waist, pulling me in front of him.

My hip brushed against him and a fevered explosion burst through the rest of my body. My chest constricted against my lungs, making each breath harder to draw, but breathing was the furthest impulse from my mind as I looked up into Mo's eyes.

My lips parted of their own accord, drawing in a soft gasp at the rush of feelings flooding my body.

Mo's hands, gentle and warm against my waist, moved to my hips, his thumbs sliding softly into place where my hip bones protruded. He pressed softly against my hips, causing my knees to buckle against the pressure of the bed behind them.

He reached for my elbows, so that I eased onto the bed. As he leaned closer, his cheek brushing against my own, he whispered in my ear, "You need to sleep."

The anticipation that had been burgeoning in my body was gone in an instant. *What a fool I am.* Had I really so misunderstood Mo? I'd been a slave to my foolish body and had completely misread him.

As he pulled away, I felt Mo pause. It was only a second. Maybe two. The pressure of his cheek against mine increased slightly. And just before he slid away, I was certain I felt the subtle warmth of Mo's lips brushing against my cheek.

I laid back and pulled the sheet into a ball across my chest, certain that if he looked, Mo would see the thundering of my heart against the walls of my chest.

He retrieved his bedroll and went into the kitchen to turn out the flame. I heard the rustling as he prepared to lay out his bedding in there.

"Mo?" I called to him across the darkened room.

"Yeah?"

"I'd feel safer if ye were in here with me." I wasn't scared. I wanted Mo as close to me as possible. And for one night, I just wanted to dwell in that desire. I wanted him to be in the same room with me. I thought of the night we'd slept head to head on the kitchen floor. How I'd awoken with my hand wrapped in Mo's. *That* was what I actually wanted, but I'd settle for feeling his presence as near as possible.

"Okay," he said.

His bare feet scuffed as he padded into the room, and a low whine of friction echoed as he dragged the armchair across the floor. The air changed when he settled in beside the bed. As my eyes adjusted to the dark, I saw his outline as he sat in the chair.

"I'm right beside you," he said.

"Thank you," I whispered. In the safety of the darkness I stared at his shadowed figure.

He leaned his head back against the chair. His breathing was even and steady. My own breath adopted the rhythm of Mo's as I lay there listening to him.

TWELVE

MAY 4, 1930

A clatter arose from the wall of the cabin outside my bed.

Mo leapt from the chair.

The hammer of the pistol clicked as he pulled it back and locked it in place.

Mo rushed to the back door, his steps quick and soundless.

The sky was still dark, and I guessed I'd been asleep for no longer than an hour or two.

Joseph stood, back to the door, as Mo pulled it open.

"What was it?" Mo hissed at Joseph.

"Didn't see no'one. Came from over there." Joseph jerked his chin toward the same location I'd thought someone had been watching us from earlier.

"Stay here," Mo commanded as he slipped from the door. Branches snapped as they circled the cabin in the dark, the low murmur of their voices carried in the night as they inspected the area surrounding the cabin.

"What was it?" I demanded as Mo reentered the cabin.

"Didn't see anything. Might have just been an animal. Joseph's gonna stay out there. We're fine."

His reassurance would have been comforting if he hadn't

immediately wedged a chair solidly under the knob.

"I'll be right beside you."

I pulled aside the blanket hanging over the kitchen window. Some impulse deep within me thought if I looked out the window, I'd see something both Joseph and Mo had overlooked.

Joseph glanced at the movement and nodded when he saw that was me.

I squinted my eyes, trying to focus beyond the limits of the darkness. I searched for any change in color or some fine movement nobody else had been able to discern. There was nothing but darkness and shadow.

"Deirdre," Mo said. "There's nothing. Go back to bed."

And yet I couldn't force myself to drop the blanket and walk away. It was as though danger lurked outside, leering at me from the dark, and I wanted it to know that I saw it too. That I wouldn't cower to it.

Mo came up behind me. He placed his hand softly on my belly and pulled me back until I was forced to let the blanket drop back into place.

I leaned into him, feeling the comfort of his presence. I'd been living in fear and uncertainty for so many weeks now. Mo was strong, soft and warm against me. He felt like safety, a feeling I hadn't felt in a very long time.

"I'm scared," I whispered. The honesty slipping out of me from so many hidden truths.

He pulled me tighter against him. I felt his head lean into mine. "I know," he whispered.

I turned toward him. The outline of his face was barely visible in the darkened interior of the cabin.

His breath hitched, and his chest expanded as he drew in the breath. He kept his arm wrapped around me. His fingers fanned out and then dug gently into my lower back, pulling me toward him.

I trailed one hand along Mo's arm, feeling the definition of his muscles as they crested and dipped below my palm. My palm traveled to his shoulders before resting high on his back. I let the fingers from my other hand drift along his strong jawline, the stubble on his face slightly rigid, but with a smooth quality that didn't poke at my skin. The hollow of his cheek was subtle, his cheekbones well defined. I let my open palm rest against his face, and he leaned into it.

The rise and fall of his chest against my own increased in its rate and depth.

I pressed against him, wanting every part of my body to be in contact with his. Wanting to miss nothing.

The hand Mo held against my lower back flattened and traveled down before clutching and pulling me tighter into him.

I snaked my arm around his shoulders. My other hand served as a beacon, letting me know exactly where Mo's face was in relation to my own. The heat of his face in my palm intensified. My thumb found the soft divet under his lower lip, then followed it up and across his velvety mouth.

We molded against each other.

My mouth, only inches away from his, was greedy in anticipation. My thumb had barely completed its pass across his lip before I pressed a kiss against the welcoming mouth.

Mo leaned into me, and I clung in desperation., pulling him ever tighter against me.

My gasping breaths drove on his own desperation. My hands traveled along Mo's body, touching every bit of him that had ever drawn my attention in the daylight. Here, in the dark of the night and spurred by the greed of pure desire, I'd found the safety to explore my most carnal impulses.

And it seemed Mo was intent on fulfilling the same urges.

The presence of the counter prevented Mo from pushing me any further back.

I gasped as his hands slid to the back of my thighs and he lifted me onto the counter and leaned into me. His hands slid under my dress, the sharp magnetic pull of my bare skin responding to his touch was nearly too much to endure.

Mo's hands slid over my hips and dug into my flesh as he pulled me even tighter against him.

I stretched my hands, reaching over his shoulders and down his back. I grasped at his shirt, pulling it over his head.

Mo lifted his arms as I relieved him of the thin material that separated me from his bare skin. I threw the shirt into the dark of the room, unconcerned with where it landed or how it would appear to anyone seeing the cast-off clothing. The only thing that mattered, the only thing I was concerned with, was feeling Mo's bare skin against me.

Mo turned his attention to the buttons along the front of my dress. His fingers traced the hollow of my neck and down my chest, they lingered for seconds at the locket hanging from my neck before exploring further.

My mouth was demanding in its attention to his own. My lips began to feel raw and bruised, but I couldn't—no, I wouldn't—pull away from his kisses.

My fingers strayed to Mo's hair, locking themselves around his curls. I pulled away from him, giving myself the time to take one gasping breath before I released the pressure and collapsed back into him.

Mo's weight shifted, and he lifted me.

I clung to him, my arms and legs wrapped around him as he lifted me from the counter and turned.

He carried me into the front room, never breaking the rhythm of our kisses.

My heart thundered in anticipation as he laid me on the bed and lowered himself onto me. The path of his hands, and then his kisses, was electrifying. I arched into him, craving more, grasping at him with a greed that felt as though it would never be satisfied.

The intensity of our desperate attention to each other seemed to last for hours. I was exhausted and breathless when I finally collapsed against Mo's chest in the early hours of the morning. My fingers traced the contours of his chest and abdomen as I listened to the beat of his heart and the raspy sounds of his breaths as they were drawn deep into his chest.

I tried to hold onto the magic of our night together, but guilt began to scratch at my mind. Sleeping with Mo was the farthest thing from my reason for being here. How had I let myself give in to lustful impulses? I tried to assuage my guilt with the rational that I was simply relieving myself of the tension and frustration that had built up. I'd needed a few minutes—or hours—to dwell in a world without the concerns of the Moret family.

Mo's fingers traveled the length of my spine before settling against my ribs. Heat radiated from every place where my body came into contact with him, relaxing my muscles. Sleep played heavily in my mind and I welcomed its embrace.

When I awoke, Mo slept in the chair beside me. He was fully clothed, and the pistol rested against his leg, his hand gripped around it even in sleep.

I pulled the sheet around me as I slipped from the bed and tiptoed to the wardrobe. I pulled a clean dress out and slipped it over my head, tucking my locket into the neckline. With a peek over my shoulder to ensure Mo was still sleeping, I retrieved my blade and strapped it to my thigh. I walked barefoot into the kitchen and peaked through the window. Joseph stood on the path, smoking a cigarette and eying the periphery of the cabin. He raised his chin in greeting when he saw me and headed toward the door.

Damn it. I was hoping for just a little more time to dwell in this world that only consisted of Mo, myself, and what had happened between us last night. I glanced over my shoulder at Mo as I slipped the chair from under the knob. In that second, I committed this moment, this part of time, to my memory.

Joseph lumbered into the kitchen. "Mornin'. I still ain't got no idea what that was last night. Ain't seen or heard a thing the rest of the night."

He sat at the table as I started the water for coffee. "Musta been *loup rougarou*, eh, Mo?"

Mo stepped into the kitchen, tucking the pistol into the back of his pants. He cast a quick glance at me before he was distracted by Joseph's ongoing theories about what had caused the noise. "It wasn't no *rougarou*," he growled at Joseph.

"What's a *rougarou*?" I'd never heard of such a thing.

Joseph grew highly animated as he described the legend of the half wolf creature that prowls the swamps and preys on those who don't follow the rules. It was apparent that Joseph had no idea—nor suspicions—about what had happened between Mo and I last night. He was like a young boy describing his greatest dream, only Joseph's involved some vengeful creature prowling about the cabin I slept in. The story, no matter how preposterous, did nothing to temper my unease.

After eating the breakfast I had prepared them, Joseph slipped into the front room to sleep.

I pulled the curtain between the two rooms and returned to the table to clear my own dishes.

As I stepped beside Mo and reached for my dish, I felt his hand slide up the back of my thigh. He looked up at me as his hand came to a rest, just shy of an indecent location.

My body responded immediately. My heart raced, and I reached for his cheek, leaning down to kiss him. He smelled like fresh coffee and sun-warmed skin.

He pulled me into his lap and his hand traveled the length

of my body from my thigh to my neck, cupping it gently as he pulled me into the heat of another kiss.

"We can't let Joseph see this," I whispered.

"I know. I just needed one more. I want to make sure we're okay."

I slipped from his lap and onto my own chair in case Joseph were to come in—or one of the Moret gang were to show up.

"Why wouldn't we be okay?"

He stammered. "Because of, well, last night. I didn't intend to—"

I reached for his hand in reassurance. "Neither did I, but it happened. You didn't do anything I didn't want to do, Mo. And I'm not about to apologize. I don't expect you to either."

"It's a problem, though. I mean, it could become a problem. A big one."

"With Jack?"

He nodded.

"I'm not Jack's lover. I never was and never intended to be."

"I know. But that ain't how he sees it." He looked up, resignation and even fear clouding his usually bright eyes. "It's a problem."

He was right. I knew that. I tried to stay busy, so I wouldn't think about the implications of Jack thinking I'd betrayed him. Of thinking that Mo had betrayed him.

This was most definitely a problem.

My mind turned to the creature Joseph had described. The entire time he'd been relaying the legend, I'd imagined one person who personified such a frightening beast. I had no doubt that a rougarou might resemble Jack Moret. And Mo and I had just broken a rule set by him.

A very big problem, indeed.

THIRTEEN

Word trickled to Mo about the increasing number of Moret customers the Granger Gang had begun to supply.

Tim became a regular visitor to the cabin. Three times a week, he showed up with more bad news for Mo. "We can't get near the liquor with the revenuers on our backs. And we can't get the liquor to our customers because they're too scared to set up a drop when one of us already been busted."

"And what about Jack?"

"Nobody knows where he is, Mo. Or they ain't sayin'."

I didn't know where Jack Moret was, but I was certain I knew where he'd been. Who else would be lurking around the cabin?

Every time Tim left, Mo would be left in a foul mood. He'd taken to spending hours on the front porch watching the tides and mulling over his predicament.

"Is it so bad that I just want to prove to my dad that I can be trusted to take over the business?"

We were watching the sun set. Joseph was at the dock, fishing. He'd started to venture farther from the house as his wound healed.

I offered a sympathetic look but didn't say anything.

A short laugh escaped him, and he squinted against the sun's rays. "I know. It ain't like taking over a family store or nothin', but I always thought that one day, if I tried hard enough, I'd prove he could trust me."

Mo and I had settled into a more open manner of talking since our night together. We were bonded now, though we didn't give in to the pull we felt for each other. Even without the ongoing physical act, we had a connection we didn't have before.

"Why doesn't your dad trust ye? It's obvious to me that you'll do whatever it takes for your family. You're not the one who ran away and let yer dad take the fall. Sure, you've been in hiding, but in plain sight, to be honest. Every member of the Moret gang—as well as everyone in Cleric's Cove—know where ye are. Nobody can say that about yer uncle."

Mo sighed. He leaned back and kicked an ankle over his knee, pulling at the hem of his pants. "I made some decisions my pére didn't like."

I nearly lost my breathe. Was Mo about to reveal information that I could benefit from? I fought to maintain an unaffected voice as I asked, "Like what?"

He turned his attention to the frayed threads that hung from his pant leg. "I did some things. Things I regret. My pére— and Jack—think if I have regrets, I'm too soft to be in charge."

"There's nothing wrong with regret."

"There is if it stops you from doin' what needs done. If it gets in the way of business."

My voice was a whisper on the breeze. I wasn't even certain he heard me ask, "Have you ever killed anyone?"

He stood up suddenly. "That's enough of that kind of talk. I'm gonna go see what Joseph's caught for dinner."

I watched him walk away. My thoughts churning, wondering what things Mo had done and regretted. I knew from our first meeting that he'd beaten at least one person. Badly, based on the extent of his own injuries. I knew that it hadn't been the first time. Had he done worse? Had he killed? Finn's face floated across my vision and I shuddered.

Shame washed over me, it had become a near constant companion. I'd come here to avenge my brother, a plan that was admittedly a lofty one in hindsight. I'd had no idea what it would take to get near Claude Moret. I'd had no idea how big his organization was. I hadn't planned on Claude being in jail— or on Jack. I certainly hadn't planned on Mo.

Now that I'd found myself so deeply enmeshed in this ridiculous plan of mine, I realized there was no easy way out.

How could I run from Jack Moret if I didn't know where he was? He wasn't far, I knew that. Each time I felt the shudder of evil on the wind, I knew he was somewhere close. He was the presence in the trees. He came at night as well as the day. Even though we never spoke the words, I knew he was there and Mo knew it as well. I suspected that even Joseph had begun to suspect the feeling we had of being watched was a legitimate one.

"Catfish!" Joseph held up the fish he and Mo had cleaned as he approached the porch.

Mo remained at the dock, cleaning the mess they'd left behind.

My skin prickled. *It's just my nerves*, I rationalized. I was just thinking about Jack and now my mind is playing tricks on me.

Joseph paused and looked toward the tree line, his eyes narrowed as they searched.

I stepped to the edge of the porch to follow his gaze. I nearly jumped as something shifted in the depths of the overgrowth.

Joseph's head spun to me as he looked for confirmation that we'd both seen the same thing.

Mo came up behind Joseph and looked between us. "What?"

"Nothing," Joseph answered. He handed his catch to Mo and clutched at his abdomen, leaning into the wound. "I think I pulled somethin' is all. Must overdone it."

Mo accepted the fish and grabbed Joseph by the elbow, helping him to the porch.

I followed them in. Closing the door behind me.

The blankets had been pulled back from the windows earlier in the day. It would be easy for anyone to see in.

"Sit down," Mo told Joseph.

They sat at the table and I stood at the counter, moving about as if I was busy preparing a meal.

"Someone's outside," Joseph said. "We both saw him. In the trees."

"Who was it?"

"Couldn't tell. Deirdre?"

"It was Jack," I said without looking to them. I hadn't seen him, but I knew. And I was engulfed in fear. I felt his eyes on me still. I grabbed a handful of carrots and sliced them into microscopic slices.

Joseph let out a long breath. "I was afraid of that. Mo, I didn't say anythin' before, but Tim's boy mentioned to me that someone's been messin' with Jack's woman. I thought he meant his wife. Then Leonie mentioned that Deirdre is Jack's—"

I spun on him, knife in hand. "I *am not!*"

Joseph raised his hands up as if warding me off.

"Hey." Mo moved on me, deftly wrenching the knife from my grip before I realized what had happened. He pointed the knife in Joseph's direction as he reclaimed his seat. "Watch what ya say," he warned.

"I never thought so before," Joseph said apologetically. "But it makes sense. I been finding flowers on the front porch near ev'ry mornin'. They gotta be for you. Ain' nobody gonna bring me flowers. Mo had me get rid of 'em."

"What?" I was as appalled by the fact that someone had been leaving flowers as by the fact that it had been hidden from me.

Mo shook his head at Joseph's admission and cast him a scathing look. "I didn't want to upset you. I figured if you knew someone was sneakin' around at night, it'd put you more on edge."

"But it don't make sense for Jack to be mad," Joseph said. He used his thumb to point from himself to Mo. "Neither of us'd dare mess with you."

Mo's eyes dropped, and his skin flushed briefly.

I looked at Joseph and was confident he hadn't noticed Mo's look of guilt.

"I'm not Jack's girl," I said again. "It wouldn't matter if ye were both messin' with me. It's not Jack's business."

"But he thinks you are," they both said.

I turned to the basin. Frustration was trying to rally my tears to join it. I focused on blinking each one away as it appeared.

"It's not safe here," I said. "We're not safe here."

"It's too late to go now," Joseph said. "There's only an hour of daylight left. We don't know where Jack actually is or if he's got people watchin' us."

"First thing. Before sun-up," Mo said.

Joseph nodded. A plan they both seemed to understand without having to put voice to it had been put into play.

All I understood of it was that we were leaving. But I'd have to stay here one more night.

CHAPTER

FOURTEEN

MAY 8 TO MAY 9, 1930

With the blankets covering the windows and kitchen chairs lodged firmly under the door knobs we turned out the lights.

"It ain't gonna stop nobody from gettin' in, but it'll slow them down until I can get a shot off," Joseph joked. He laid a bedroll on the kitchen floor and groaned as he strained to get down and comfortable.

Mo placed a candle on the small table across the room and assumed his usual position in the armchair beside my bed.

Within minutes, Joseph's breathing grew heavy and his snoring rattled throughout the house.

"Do you trust me?" Mo whispered.

I considered his question for several seconds, unsure how to answer. The dark recesses of my brain still harbored doubts about the kind of person Mo Moret really was. I'd given myself to him completely one night when I'd been desperate to forget the fear and pain that plagued me for months. At that moment I'd trusted him, but everything I'd seen and experienced since leaving New Orleans reminded me I was ill prepared to survive amongst the Morets. And he *was* a Moret.

107

"Yes," my heart voiced what my good sense doubted. I reached for his hand and pulled him until he relented and came to lie beside me.

He wrapped his arms around me. "I'm going to do everything I can to get you away from here. Out of Jack's reach."

"What about you?"

"What about me? I belong here. There ain't no away for me."

"How can you think like that? Your dad and uncle were content to stand by and watch you be killed over a disagreement of some sort. How can you *not want* escape them?"

"I'm a Moret. I'm expected to live and die like one."

I shuddered at the idea of being that obligated to your family. But hadn't I felt the same obligation? I'd been determined to avenge Finn or die trying. That's why I'd approached Jack, seduced him, and let bring me into the bayou. Yet I'd wavered in my plan, in my dedication to my own family. From the moment I met Mo, my resolve to avenge my family and destroy the Morets began to crumble.

Mo is different.

I had no doubt that he was the opposite of everything Jack and Claude revered. How could a person who was so protective of me, someone he'd just met, be capable of hurting others? I pressed my forehead against his chest and leaned into the safety of his embrace.

But he did stab Joseph. And he'd beaten at least one other person.

The question that weighed heavy in my chest now bubbled to the surface, the one he'd refused to answer down on the dock. Without looking up into his eyes, I whispered it into the space between us. "Mo, have you ever killed anyone?" *Please say no.*

His body tensed. He drew in a breath, held it for several seconds and then let it slowly seep from him.

Please say no.

"I've done a lot of things, Deirdre."

He didn't say "No."

"But, have you killed?" My heart raced, but I was unable to move, frozen in place by fear. Fear of what Mo would say and that I already knew the answer even if he *wouldn't* say it. Fear of what a tremendous fool I'd been for believing in Mo Moret.

"Ev'ry bad thing I did was for a good reason. I told you I've done things I regret. I was honest 'bout that." He lifted himself onto one arm, his face hovering just above me. He brushed my hair aside and kissed me gently as he cupped my face.

My breath refused to come except in a short ragged staccato. I barely registered the soft kiss he placed on my forehead as he rolled away from me and slipped from the bed.

The chair emitted a low groan as he resumed his guard duty. "You should sleep."

"I don't know that I can." I was well and truly an idiot and was in over my head. I had no doubt Mo had killed, which meant he was capable of anything. I'd put my trust in him, and he was no better than Claude or Jack. There'd be no choice now, but for me to bide my time until I could escape from the Morets and tell the authorities everything I knew about them.

I rolled to my back, exhaustion and heartbreak weighing heavily in my mind. I was a fool. I'd let myself fall in love with Mo and, although he hadn't said the words, he'd all but admitted that he was a murderer. He was a Moret through and through. But even with that knowledge, I didn't hate him.

My fingers found the locket and played with it, finding the familiar ridges. It tumbled about my fingertips in a natural rhythm established long ago. I lifted it, feeling the smooth edge against my lips as I blew a silent kiss against it. For Mum and Da, and for Finn. *I'm sorry I lost focus. That I failed you,* I silently begged for their forgiveness.

The links of the chain zipped as I pulled the locket to one side and then the other.

"It's special, I take it. Your necklace."

I jumped. *What a fool*, I thought. I'd pulled the locket from my collar without thought. "Yes. From me mum."

"I noticed it, the uh, the other night."

I imagined the blush coloring Mo's cheeks, matched my own cheeks at the recollection of our night together.

"It's my one thing. The thing I can't bear to live without. It used to have a photograph of my family, but that's long gone now."

"When was the last time you saw her?" His whisper was soft.

I nearly choked on the constriction in my throat. "Two months before I came to Cleric's Cove. She passed."

"And your other family?"

"My father passed shortly before her. Tuberculosis."

A heavy pause hung in the small space between us. My mind spun into a flurry of thoughts as I anticipated further questions about my family. What should I say to him? Do I claim to be an only child? Should I confess that I had a brother?

Mo shifted in his chair. Then he shifted again. He sat up and moved to the edge of the chair.

The soft peach-colored glow of the candle danced on the far wall. The shadows of the cabin seemed ominous and prepared to encroach on me at any minute.

The pistol was in Mo's hand, but hanging in a loose grip. "And your brother? Finn was his name. He *was* your brother, right?"

I scrambled in the bed, sitting up and pushing so that my back was against the wall. Mo knew. He knew that Finn was my brother. Did Jack know? Did they already suspect why I'd come here?

"How did you know?" Fear bubbled in my head, obscuring my thoughts and any attempts at rational thinking.

"I've only come across two Irish within fifty miles of Cleric's Cove. And ya look near exactly like him."

I relaxed a little. With my secret out in the open, the stress of my ruse was lifted from my shoulders. There was only one thing to left to settle. One question left to answer.

Mo looked up. Sadness heavy on his brow. "Are ya here to get revenge for him? To get even with us?"

The breath was knocked from my chest. There was so much information in his question and yet so much was still left unsaid. If Mo suspected I was here for revenge that could only mean that Finn was, in fact, dead. It also meant that it was at the hands of the Morets and that there was a reason I'd be there seeking vengeance.

I slipped to the edge of the bed, eyeing the gun Mo held. I wondered what it would take for me to strip it from him and turn it on him. Would I get the chance to get a shot off? Would he use it on me first? I clenched my teeth as I finally posed the question. "What would I be I' vengeance for? What did ye do to me brother?"

Mo looked at me, eyes wide, brows up. He shook his head as if he couldn't believe what he was about to confess to. "I'm so sorry, Deirdre. I had no idea."

A deep burn began in my chest and lit the simmering fire in my belly. I inched closer, letting my hand slide to the edge of the bed, within inches of the gun.

"It was you? You're the reason he's gone?"

Mo nodded and then dropped his head into his free hand. "I'm sorry, Deirdre. I didn't know."

My voice raised as my throat tightened against grief. "Didn't know what? What'd ye do to Finn?"

Before he could look up I lunged. I wrenched the pistol from his hand, falling as I did so.

Mo began to charge after me.

I rolled and scrambled across the floor, bracing with my back against the kitchen doorway. I leveled the pistol at Mo and clicked the hammer into place, feeling the inevitability of what I was about to do.

With his hands up, palms facing me Mo returned to the armchair, resuming his spot at the edge of it. "Deirdre, it was an accident. I didn't hurt him on purpose."

I jabbed the gun in his direction and yelled, the fury pouring out of me. It hadn't been Claude—or even Jack—after all. It had been Mo, by his own admission, it was Mo's fault that my brother was dead. "But ye did hurt him, didn't ye? It was yer fault."

He was resigned as he nodded. "It was an accident, Deirdre. I swear."

I pressed against the door jamb pushing myself to my feet while keeping the gun leveled at Mo. "But it *was* you. You said it was you. You killed my brother."

He watched me with caution, lifting his hands out further in defense. He began to shake his head.

"How did ye do it, Mo? Did ye beat him to death? Shoot him? How?"

He looked almost sad, regret passing over his face.

The click of a gun caught my attention at the same moment I felt the hard, rigid pressure of the barrel at the back of my head. "I can't let ya do this, missy," Joseph's voice was low and dangerous.

The barrel of his gun pressed harder against me as he reached around to relieve me of the pistol.

I glared at Mo, the fury in my chest burning away the tears of mourning at knowing for certain that Finn was dead.

Mo retrieved the gun from Joseph and released the hammer, sliding the gun behind his back. "Let her go," he ordered Joseph.

"But, Mo—"

His yell was explosive in the small cabin. "I said *let her go!*"

I sat on the floor, breathing ragged breaths and staring at my empty hands, the ones that, only moments ago, had held the instrument to carry out the vengeance I'd come for. I'd had a gun pointed at the man who killed my brother, and I'd failed to make use of it. As I'd always feared I might.

Joseph grunted as he lifted himself from the floor.

Mo paced across the small room, cursing under his breath. "Jesus Christ."

"Are ye goin' ta kill *me* now?" I was resigned to it. Even welcomed it. At this point, I was tired of living under the weight of revenge. I would welcome the release of the obligation that weighed so heavily on me for so many months. I was ready to be with my family and free of the world I'd never really found my place in.

"What? No. Deirdre—," he stepped toward me. "Joseph. Out!"

"But, Mo—"

"*Out. Now!*"

"Fine, but this is a bad idea. She nearly shot you once."

Mo bent and pulled me up by my hands as the back door slammed behind Joseph.

Terror kept me rigid as Mo led me to the armchair and pushed me gently so that I sat. I averted my eyes as he sat at the edge of the bed. If he pulled the gun, I preferred to be caught off guard. I was prepared to die but would rather not watch it happen.

"Deirdre, I ain't gonna hurt you."

I chanced a glimpse at him before turning my attention back to the floor boards.

"And I didn't mean to hurt Finn. When I sent him on that deal, I didn't know what was happenin'."

My thoughts tumbled. Suddenly the image I had in my head of Mo killing Finn wasn't accurate. What I thought I knew, what I'd imagined had happened, wasn't true. I looked at Mo. "What deal? What happened to him?"

"My dad needed a guy to take on a sale. He wanted one of my guys and Finn volunteered. He left yer brother with some of our associates, as collateral."

"Collateral?"

"He didn't have no intention of goin' back for him, Deirdre. I was pissed when I found out. I went to get him, but I didn't have the money Claude owed them."

Collateral? Money? I still had no idea what really happened to Finn.

"I took the fastest car we had and went after Finn in the middle of the night."

His eyes had a faraway look. He was remembering the night as it unfolded.

"Finn was the best driver." He looked up at me in earnest as if trying to convince me that it had been the best idea at the time. "He made me let him drive."

I had no doubt Finn would demand to drive. He always insisted on doing the hardest tasks. It wasn't that he thought himself better skilled than everyone else, he just never wanted anyone to be inconvenienced on his behalf.

"The Guidrys were right on our tail. We took a corner too fast and—"

Mo shook his head and pinched his eyes tight as if trying to drive the image from his memory. He looked at me, his face awash in guilt and reluctance to tell me anymore.

"And what happened?" I whispered.

He took a deep breath before he said the final words. The

ones that would put the image of my brother's death clearly in my own head. "The car turned over on its side. I was in the passenger seat and fell on him." His voice cracked. "I think I crushed him. He tried to breathe, but he couldn't."

He looked up at me again. It was clear he didn't want to say any more. Was it fear of admitting what had happened that night or fear or admitting it to me?

My voice was barely above a whisper, but it was clear and demanding. "What happened?"

Mo shook his head. "He couldn't breathe, Deirdre. He tried, but—"

"How long?"

He struggled with the answer.

"How long did my brother suffer, Mo?"

"A while. I tried to get to him. To help. But the Guidrys had caught up by then. They dragged me away from the car and started hitting me. When I woke up the sun was nearly coming up. It'd been a while I guessed—maybe an hour. Finn was still breathing, but only barely, and he wouldn't wake up. He only took a few more breaths."

The bottom dropped out of my world. My brother, sweet, funny, and willing to do anything to help ease the burden of others, had struggled to breath for an hour while Mo was beaten and unconscious. When Finn's end finally came, he'd only had the son of the man who'd sent him to his death to see him into the light of his last day on earth.

My stomach roiled and I wretched.

Mo slid across the floor and knelt in front of me. "Deirdre, I am so—"

"No!" I yelled and slid around him, standing and crossing the distance of the small room. I wrapped my arms around my waist as I paced. I felt caged, trapped in a web that had been spun by the Morets. I wanted to cry for my brother and rage against Claude and Jack. I wanted to scream at Mo. He was as guilty as his father simply because he was a Moret, and Finn had obviously trusted him. And yet I was furious because Mo really wasn't at fault. He'd risked his life—and his father's disapproval—to retrieve Finn from the Guidrys. In doing so, he'd unwittingly become the cause of Finn's death. "You don't get to tell me you're sorry. You knew. You knew who I was and you—"

A new wave of nausea gripped me as I thought of our night together. I shoved at Mo, my fists hitting his chest. "You knew who I was and you let me... you and I... we—"

I gestured to the bed and fury overtook me, and I lunged at Mo, fists connecting soundly with his head.

My anger towards Mo was matched only with that for my own stupidity. I'd walked into the Moret's world, thinking I was one step ahead of them, but I hadn't been fooling anyone other than myself.

He slipped back, swinging his arms to block mine, and then trapped them as he wrapped me tightly against him. With his chest to my back, I tried to throw my head back, hoping for the satisfying crunch of his nose against my skull. But Mo anticipated my attack and pressed his head against mine so that I couldn't get the momentum necessary to do damage.

I kicked and struggled. "You bastard."

He held fast, and my body began to give out after several minutes of struggling against him. My breaths were deep and gasping when I finally collapsed in exhaustion. As weakened as I was though, I refused to let Mo see me cry.

"You promised that nobody would hurt me. You wouldn't let anyone hurt me," I said while struggling to regain my breath against the tension of Mo's arms.

His voice was low and strained as he answered, "I *won't* let anyone hurt you."

"*You* hurt me, Mo," I growled at him.

His grip loosened as he relaxed against me. The veracity of my statement knocking the fight from him. "You're right."

Mo released me, and I heard his footsteps crossing the room.

I leaned against the wall, forehead against the firm, cool wood. I took several deep gasps, gaining control of my breath as well as my impulses. I rolled so that I was facing Mo.

He leaned against the wall by the front door. "Joseph and I'll get you out of here. Make sure you're safe. And then we'll never be able to hurt you again. *I'll* never be able to hurt you again."

I nodded. There was nothing I wanted right then, but to be away from the Moret family and everyone they controlled.

Mo walked into the kitchen. I heard the door open and he said, "Stay in here with her. I'll take watch."

Joseph came into the room and slid the armchair against the front door before he slumped into it. He laid the shotgun across his lap and raised his brows at me.

There was no misunderstanding. Joseph was eager to shoot me should I have any inclinations toward getting out of hand again.

"I need water," I told him.

He shrugged his shoulders. "Then git some."

Mo was at the table loading a rifle as I entered. He stepped through the back door as I finished my drink. He stopped and looked at me. His voice was low as he said, "I never intended to hurt you."

He pulled the door closed. His steps echoed on the wooden porch.

I returned to the front room and fell on the bed, pulling the sheet over my head to escape the world in which Finn was dead and Mo was responsible.

FIFTEEN

The inky black of night had barely given way to the lavender skies of early morning when Mo came back into the cabin.

"We need to go," Mo said.

"What's up?" Joseph lolled about in the chair, sleep rolling off him slowly. He hefted himself up, gun at the ready. "What's going on?"

"We need to get goin'. Gather up now." Mo moved about the small room with urgent steps. His face was drawn tight. Each time he passed a window he lifted the blanket and searched the outside for signs of danger.

His heightened sense of urgency wasn't just because he felt it was time to go. Mo had either heard or seen something or felt a sense of dread that had spurred him to action.

The same dark knot pulled at my belly.

I grabbed my bag and pulled the shawl from it. I rolled my blanket quickly and stuffed it in before drawing the closure tight, knotting the rope.

Joseph was at the table emptying bullets into his pockets.

"Let's go," I urged. Each moment we were in the cabin

suddenly felt more dangerous. Perhaps it was just my desire to get away from the Morets. I had to distance myself from this nightmare I'd clambered to insert myself into.

"We're gonna take the boat all the way over to Catahoula Bay," Mo told Joseph as he reached for the door.

"Are you crazy?"

Mo stood taller, establishing himself as the person in charge of decisions. "I got someone outside Larose, and I got a car stashed there. We can get her that far at least."

He turned to me. "Then you go north or west. Wherever you want. I ain't gonna stop you."

Some part of by brain whispered a question I wouldn't ask on my own. *Does he want to stop me?*

I nodded. I wrapped myself in the shawl and slung the bag over my shoulder.

Mo stopped at the front door. "We go straight out to the boat. Once we walk out this door we aint comin' back. You got ev'rything?"

I nodded and took a deep breath as Mo turned the knob.

The chill in the early morning air enveloped me and seeped into my pores. My heart pounded in anticipation. I was finally going to be free of the Moret family and my ridiculous plan for vengeance.

I'd be free to go anywhere. Maybe I'd go to California. Thoughts of a new life buoyed my spirit and quickened my pace.

Mo pulled me by the hand as we made our way toward the dock.

How was it that the man leading me to salvation had witnessed Finn's destruction? *Not just a witness, he helped bring it about. He's a Moret, after all.*

My skin betrayed me, sending electricity from everywhere that made contact with Mo.

He didn't kill Finn on purpose, the whispers chastised me. *He was trying to save him.*

But everything that happened was a result of the Morets, and I'd be better off putting as much distance as possible between myself and them.

Joseph ran ahead and pushed the boat from the shore into the lake. "Oh shit."

He turned to us then cast a look along the tree line.

As Mo and I reached the boat I saw what Joseph meant. There were holes in the sides and the bateau was taking on water.

"Let's go." Mo spun around, pulling me behind him.

I nearly fell as my feet slipped on the damp grass.

We circled the cabin and got on the trail that led into Cleric's Cove.

My lungs were burning, and my legs felt numb as I was pulled along at Mo's pace. Joseph nipped at my heels.

We burst into the clearing and headed toward the houses.

A burst of gunshots filled the air. I screamed in time with the birds who burst from the tree tops, startled from their slumber.

Mo spun and wrapped himself around me, pushing me to the ground and shielding me as I struggled to see where the shots had come from.

A faint ringing sounded in my ears and grew louder.

Mo's weight lifted from me and I felt his hands lifting and moving me. His voice was distant as he asked, "Are you hurt?"

I looked up at him. I recognized his words but couldn't seem to make sense of them or form a reply.

It was several seconds before my brain caught up with everything that was happening in Cleric's Cove.

Mo pulled me to my feet and I heard a humming sound in

the distance. I looked about the clearing. *How strange that nobody's come out of the houses*, I thought.

The humming grew louder. It was the sound of car engines.

Mo pulled me in the direction of the lake.

Before we'd left the clearing, a car appeared in our path. And then another. Several men jumped from the cars as they pulled to a stop on each side of us.

Mo stopped short at the sight of the guns. He positioned himself in front of me and held his hands up in surrender.

"Where ya headed, Mo?" One of the men leered at us.

"I think he's makin' a run for it. With my girl." I spun around to see Jack Moret step through the doorway and out of Leonie's house.

My mouth ran dry, and I struggled for breath. I reached for the blade on my thigh. *My knife!* In the rush I'd forgotten to retrieve it from the wardrobe. A chasm opened in my stomach, the greatest danger I'd ever known had just reappeared. All senses drained from my body, starting at my head. I was alone, nobody in the world would defend me against Jack Moret. Certainly, nobody in Cleric's Cove.

Leonie's eyes were dull as she pushed her door closed behind Jack. How long had he been there with her? It didn't matter.

Jack's mouth spread into a sinister smile as he neared us.

Mo turned slightly, placing himself directly between Jack and me.

A look of feigned curiosity settled into Jack's face. "What's this? Certainly, my *nephew* ain't tryin' to keep me from my girl?"

"Look, Jack—"

Jack gestured and one of the men stepped forward before Mo could say more. *Crack!*

The sound of the gun striking the side of Mo's head caused

me to startle. I yelled without thought and then clasped my hands across my traitorous mouth.

Mo was driven to one knee by the blow. He stammered a bit and then pressed his hands to his knee and forced himself up to standing. He faced his uncle, providing a wall between Jack and myself.

Jack reached a hand toward the man who'd struck Mo. The beefy thug handed over his gun.

Jack's steps were slow and deliberate as he circled us.

I cast a glance over my shoulder. Twenty yards away Joseph lay on the ground propped on one elbow, two men standing over him with guns pointed only inches above him.

"Mr. Moret," I began, unsure of what I could say, but determined to try anything to ensure Mo and Joseph walked away from this confrontation.

"*Mister* Moret?" He was affronted, and his anger enhanced. He drove the gun into Mo's abdomen and then swung it at his head again. "Is that what she calls you, *Junior*? Is that the name she screams when you're together?"

My heart dropped, and a sickening realization came over me. The only way to survive this was same way I'd gotten in to it. I shook off my repulsion at the thought of being near Jack Moret and resumed the identity that had captured his attention in the first place. It was time to become the alluring immigrant he'd thought was destined to become his lover.

"Jack," I said. My voice was soft, eyes widened in innocence. I stood with one hip kicked forward, but only slightly. Enticing, not indecent. I let my brogue come on thick, the way he liked it. "He was only lookin' after me. Fer you. I was afraid I'd never see ye again. I've been waitin' so long."

My first steps toward him were hesitant. My breaths hitched with each step, certain it would be my last. I forced my eyes to play the game. Never looking at where Mo knelt on the ground at Jack's feet. I cast a shy glance at Jack's face, then flicked to his chest. I reached my hand, letting my fingertips tickle across the surface of his wrist, the one that held the gun. The one that wasn't splattered with flecks of Mo's blood.

I stopped beside Jack, letting my breast linger against his arm, only long enough for him to take notice. I lifted my gaze to his again. My voice was a mixture of sultry enticement and fear. "I was scared, Jack. I thought ye'd left me. Or worse, that ye'd been hurt."

Uncertainty flickered in his eyes and then doubt.

I seized the last moment possible. I stepped in front of him and reached up, placing my hands on each side of his face. I looked intently into his eyes and pulled him to me for a soft, lingering kiss. Though the kiss was chaste, I made sure to press my body against his just enough that he'd feel the curves of my body.

Jack responded, his hands circling behind me, lingering low on my back.

As I pulled away I held his gaze, reading into his eyes.

I'd done it. I was certain that Jack Moret believed that I was still his and that neither Mo nor Joseph had been a threat to his claim. I smiled at him. "We should go," I urged.

"Yeah," he said. His voice was a mix of resignation and lingering lust.

I wrapped my fingers around his and tugged him, eager to move him away from Mo. Wherever he was taking me, I'd face that on my own.

As I stepped, Mo looked up, I saw the crimson path of blood flowing from the split next to his eye. I blinked hard against the image. When I opened my eyes, Jack was looking directly at me, a storm brewing in his eyes.

"Take care of them both," he said. He gripped my upper arm and yanked me so that I had no choice but to follow him.

The gunshots were immediate.

I spun around as Joseph fell back against the ground.

"No," I screamed.

Dull thuds reverberated as two of the men turned on Mo, driving punches into his face as Mo tried to fend them off.

"They didn't do anything," I begged, pulling against Jack's grip.

He didn't say a word. His brow was set in fury and determination.

The bruising on my arm was deep and aching, but I pulled against him still. "No, Jack. Please. You have to believe me."

He drove me forward, shoving me into a car and climbing in behind me. The driver took off immediately.

I realized the more I begged on behalf of Mo, the more evident it was that I cared what happened to him, and the more likely it was that he'd have Mo killed.

The fight drained from me and I focused on taking in my surroundings. I paid attention to every road the driver took.

It was less than ten minutes before we pulled up to an old house in a clearing. The place seemed to be abandoned, windows had boards nailed across them. Pieces of the porch had fallen, and boards hung dangerously, looking as if they'd join their fallen cohorts any day now.

The driver pulled around the back where two other cars were parked.

Jack gripped my upper arm again and drug me from the car. He didn't pause as he pulled me up the steps and into the house.

We came in through what had once been a kitchen.

"Jack!" Several people called in surprise as he entered the room.

From the other room I heard more people shuffling to come in and confirm that it was, indeed Jack.

Jack pushed me through the crowd of men. I recognized a few from the cabin. They'd been there after Claude Moret was arrested and Jack had run away. They were more surprised to see me than the others.

Jack ignored their questions as he pushed me down the hall through a splintered doorway. In the room was an unmade bed, stained wash basin and lopsided wooden chair. The wooden slats in the floor had been worn with age and some had been chewed through by rodents

"Sit!" Jack commanded as he shoved me toward the chair.

I did, looking about the room for anything I could use to defend myself against him. The room was sparse. There was nothing here.

Jack shrugged his jacket off and called for someone to bring him rope.

Within minutes I was secured to the chair.

There was a knock at the door. "What?"

A wiry man in a bowler hat entered. It seemed this was the last pace he wanted to be. His hands nervously clutched at the hem of his vest and he shifted his weight from foot to foot as he addressed Jack. "Teddy sent a message. Came through last night. It's Bastienne, Jack. She ain't doin' good."

Jack was upon the poor man before the last word left his mouth. "What's wrong with her?"

The man flinched. "They din't say, Jack. Just said to tell ya ta git home quick."

"Damn it!" Jack stormed from the room.

From the back of the house, the engine of a car roared to life followed by the clatter of dirt flung from spinning tires as the car sped from behind the house.

I looked at the man, my mouth open in surprise. I tried to think quickly. "Can you loosen the ropes a bit? They're very tight."

The man shook his head and backed to the door as if he thought I might attack him.

"Please," I called. How would I even get away if I could get free from the chair? It was too far to run to the covering of trees. There were cars, but I wasn't much of a driver and had no clue where to find the keys.

Where would I even go if I *could* get away?

I was certain I could get back to the cabin, but why? Joseph was dead. It was likely that Mo had been killed as well. My throat constricted and burned as I swallowed away the thought.

He was different.

In every way Mo Moret had been different.

I struggled against the ropes until they chaffed at my wrists and ankles. Jack had done a solid job of securing me.

I listened for clues from the other room. It seemed several people were sleeping there, but they were very cautious in keeping their voices lowered. Nothing but a mumble of indistinct voices reached me.

Hours after the sun had gone down and darkness engulfed the room, the lights of a car appeared.

I squinted against the sudden and invasive light. My eyes exploded in bursts of starlight and globes behind my closed lids.

Pounding steps erupted from the outer steps, followed by the click of boot heels hurrying down the hall toward the room I was in.

I braced for the worst possible outcome.

The door flew open and a boy, several years younger than I, burst in, chest heaving. "You the healer?"

I was startled that I was suddenly not a captive, but back to being regarded as a healer. "My dad sent me after ya. My mére needs help."

"Your dad?"

He crossed the room and untied my binds. "Jack Moret," he said.

With a house full of Moret lackies, I didn't dare try to escape, so I followed the boy down the hall. A man I recognized from the cabin, Davey if I remembered right, pointed a pistol at me. "Don't do nothin' stupid. Mrs. Moret needs help."

I nodded. The sudden change of situation—in addition to all the other events of the day—had rendered me silent long before the gun. It was probably for the best, I figured. I couldn't seem to keep myself out of trouble as it was.

Before we reached the door, another man stepped in our path. "I'm s'posed to make sure ya have your healin' stuff. Where is it?"

"Um, at the cabin. By the lake."

"What d'ya need?" he demanded.

"Well, I don't know. What's wrong with her?"

He gave me a sour look. "Well if I knew that *I'd* be the doctor, and we wouldn't have need for you. Ain't that right?"

"Everything, then. If I don't know what's wrong with her, I'll need it all. It's on the shelves in the kitchen. And don't break the jars."

He nodded and turned to the door.

Davey nodded and waved me on with the gun.

The boy circled his finger impatiently. "Let's go."

"What's yer mum's name?" I asked when we were in the car.

"Why?" He was distrustful as I imagined a Moret would be raised to be.

"I like to refer to my patients by their names. It puts them at ease, which makes it easier fer me to treat them."

He nodded, satisfied with my explanation. "Her name's Bastienne."

And this must be Teddy, I thought.

Teddy turned the car onto a long, tree lined drive, ending in front of a large house. The light from inside glowed yellow against the indigo night.

"Hurry up," Teddy ordered. He rushed from the car himself, leaving the door open.

From behind the house, I heard the soft nickering of horses. Hounds called to each other from far away in the night. Frogs sang in the distance, echoing the steady chirp of crickets and other creatures.

I hastened my pace as I had no desire to remain outdoors. No matter how long I'd been in Louisiana nights in the bayou unnerved me.

"Up the stairs," a pinch-faced man commanded.

I climbed the steps and followed the sounds of people. As I walked in I realized very quickly I was in Jack and Bastienne Moret's bedroom.

Jack sat in an armchair in the corner. He didn't move or even acknowledge my presence.

In the bed, surrounded by women fanning her and moistening her forehead with wet cloths, lay his wife.

"The healer's here, Momma," one of the ladies said. Her belly was rounded with pregnancy. I guessed her to be twenty.

Jack Moret's wife had been suffering for a time indeed if she'd been married to him long enough to have a daughter that age.

I stepped forward and most of the ladies backed away from the bed to give me room to work.

The daughter leveled a knowing gaze at me.

"Bastienne?" I placed a hand over hers.

"You'll call her *Missus* Moret," the daughter snapped.

I nodded, consciously keeping my gaze from flickering to

Jack for even an instant. I squeezed her hand a bit tighter and said her name again. "Mrs. Moret."

She opened her eyes slowly and turned to face me. Her eyes took me in slowly. First, she studied my face, then moved down before returning to meet my eyes.

She knew exactly who I was. Or who Jack—and the rest of his people—thought me to be.

"I'm not dyin' yet. So, you just get outta my house, tramp." The crackles in her breath as she spoke told me she had fluid in her lungs. And a lot of it.

"I'm a nurse, Mrs. Moret. I'm here ta look after ye." I fell back into my thick accent. If there was one thing I'd learned about Americans, it was that they felt safer, more in control, when they were in the presence of an immigrant. If that was what it took to tend to this obviously very sick lady, I was happy to let her—and her daughter—maintain their illusion of supe-riority.

"Are ye havin' trouble breathin'?"

She turned her head, lips pursed, ignoring my question.

"She's been coughin' for three days," the daughter said and clutched at Bastienne's hand.

"Can I look at yer feet and legs?"

Bastienne didn't answer, but her daughter nodded. "Let her help, Mamma."

I pulled the sheet aside. Bastienne's legs and feet were round and tight against the skin. I ran my hands over her shins, pausing to press my fingers gently against both. As I moved my fingers further down, the imprint of the pressure I'd exerted against her remained for several seconds before the fluid pushed the indentation out. The same happened when I pressed against her feet.

I looked at one of the women hovering against the wall. "Could ye find some more pillows to put under her legs?"

She nodded and scurried off to do as requested.

"Can I feel yer tummy?" I asked and began to palpate when she agreed.

"Is she eatin' as usual?"

Her daughter shook her head. "She ain't been eatin' hardly at all. Say's she ain't hungry."

Bastienne winced as I pressed into the right upper portion of her abdomen.

"Sorry, love." I reached a hand up and felt along her neck, though I didn't have to. I could see the pulsation.

None of my assessment findings were good for Bastienne Moret. She was suffering from the final stages of heart failure. Delivering this news would not bring me a thankful reprieve from Jack—nor his daughter, I assumed.

A car arrived, and I heard the clank of my jars being carried up the stairs.

I turned as the men entered the room, boxes in hand.

"Perhaps the kitchen?" I would have far more freedom— and space—to work without the hovering hens that were gathered in the room.

I was led into the kitchen by two of the women who proceeded to place all my jars onto the counter. Then, they pulled the dried herbs out that were wrapped in cheese cloth and laid them down as well.

"I'll need a pot of water. Perhaps two." I pulled out the jars of dandelions and parsley and unwrapped the twigs of bittersweet nightshade I'd collected only days ago.

As I dropped them into the boiling water, Jack stormed into the room. He grabbed me by the wrist and shoved me against the wall.

"Are you gonna tell me what's wrong with my wife?"

I winced against the pressure of his grip. "It's her heart. It's failing her."

He looked at me with suspicion. "How do you know that?"

"Her heart isn't pumping right. It's causing fluid to accumulate in her body. That's why her legs are swollen and ye can see the force of her heart tryin' to work, here." I indicated on my neck where Bastienne's carotid artery could be seen pulsating. "The fluid is accumulating in her lungs. That's why she's havin' trouble breathing. Ye can hear the crackles when she breathes."

His distrust turned to near begging. "But you can help her, right?"

This was it. Jack would never forgive me after I said what I had to.

"I can ease her symptoms. Make her more comfortable. But I can't cure her, Jack. I'm sorry."

He pulled me toward him and slammed me back against the wall. My head cracked against the plaster and the breath knocked from me.

Jack leaned into me, pressing me further against the wall and growled in my ear. "She'd better not die."

He spun around and stormed from the room.

The ladies who'd been helping me stood wide-eyed across the room.

I inhaled deeply, forcing my lungs to cooperate with regular breathing. I pushed away from the wall and returned to the tea I had brewing.

One of the ladies, Clarisse, stepped next to me and looked into the pot. She looked about before she whispered a question that must have been burning in her brain for several minutes. "I thought bittersweet nightshade was poisonous."

I wondered if she'd let me serve Mrs. Moret the tea if I confirmed that it was poisonous. "No. Only the berries are poisonous. The twigs are a diuretic. It'll help her get rid of the fluid."

"What else is in it?"

"Dandelion and parsley. They'll do the same, help her get rid of the fluid. It's not flavorful, most natural medicinals aren't. But it does the trick."

She nodded. Satisfied with my answer. She opened the small jar and inhaled deeply. "I love the smell of parsley."

I smiled and turned my attention back to my brew.

When the tea was ready, one of the ladies carried it up to the room. "The more ye can get her to drink the better," I instructed.

I set about preparing more. It would be a long night of trying to get Bastienne Moret comfortable again.

Jack's daughter came into the kitchen. "Daddy's stomach is a bit upset. Can you make him somethin'?"

I nodded, and she turned immediately without waiting for another word.

"I'll need more water," I said over my shoulder to Clarisse.

As she took the pot to fill it I emptied half of the parsley into my pocket. I slipped the lid from a jar I'd marked with an "X" and hurriedly poured its contents into the parsley jar. I shook the green herbs together, mixing them evenly.

"What do we put in this," Clarisse asked.

"For an upset stomach, we'll need the peppermint leaves," I pointed to the proper jar.

Clarisse opened the lid and again took a deep whiff of the contents before handing it to me.

I emptied several leaves into the pot.

"And the chamomile blossoms," I pointed and Clarisse dutifully selected, removed the lid and smelled before handing it to me.

"And of course, the parsley." I held my breath as she sniffed again, afraid she'd detect the subtle difference in aroma or leaves. She noticed neither.

I paused for a moment before pouring in the contents. There

would be no going back from this decision. I was about to poison Jack Moret. I was doing it for myself. And for Joseph. And for Mo. And everyone else that Jack had ever hurt. I was doing it for Bastienne, so that she could outlive her unfaithful bastard of a husband.

With that final declaration. I poured in a third of the jar and stirred the contents of the pot. I realized I'd need something to ensure Jack would drink the tea—and that nobody else would try it."

I stirred two tablespoons of honey into the mixture and then made a grand show of pulling two pumpkin seeds from a jar, breaking them in half and dropping them in.

Cerisse accepted the spoon and stirred. "What are those for?"

"The other ingredients might cause Mr. Moret to become very, shall we say relaxed. He's a virile man, and I'm sure he wouldn't take to a decrease in his urges." I leaned into her conspiratorially. "The seeds will ensure he's as virile as he is on any other day. Maybe give him an extra bit of vim."

She giggled. "Maybe I should have a sip. My husband would be happy."

I gasped, "Oh, no. Swear you won't. The seeds can cause terrible infertility in women."

Clarisse seemed properly shocked, and I was convinced she would neither sip the tea, nor allow any of the other women to partake.

But for an extra measure I added, "Me mum was called for a woman who near bled to death from hemorrhage after just a sip." I shook my head and *tsked* at the memory. "Was tragic, she was only twenty-three and not a child."

One of the women returned for another cup of tea for Mrs. Moret. "She seems to be better, Charlatan."

I shook my head as the heifer left the kitchen.

"Perhaps ye should go up and check on Mrs. Moret," I told Clarisse. "I'm sure you've been worried about her. I'll finish up with Mr. Moret's tea and bring it up."

"What tea?" Jack loomed at the door.

My heartbeat thundered in my ears. The world slowed down, everything was happening at a painfully slow pace.

"Maybe I will go check on her," Clarisse said. Though I thought her tone was conspiratorial, as though she imagined I wanted time alone with Jack.

I returned to the stove, pulling a tea cup from the shelf as I passed. "Yer daughter said yer stomach was upset. She asked that I brew somethin' up for ye."

The pounding of my heart was thundering. Could he hear it thump against my chest? I was certain it echoed throughout the room.

I struggled to maintain a neutral demeanor. I could neither show hostility nor pleasantry to him or it'd arouse his suspicions. "It's nearly done. Have a seat and I'll pour you a cup."

Jack eased into a chair at the table.

I found a ladle and poured the tea into a cup and set it in front of Jack. I knew I wouldn't be able to pull my eyes from the cup if I stood there watching so I turned my back. My attention back to the teas brewing on the stove.

"I understand Mrs. Moret is doin' a bit better."

"Seems to be," Jack said.

I risked a glance over my shoulder, Jack was studying the cup, but I wasn't sure if he'd taken a drink of it yet.

"I've just about finished another batch. Perhaps you can take her another cup when you go back up?"

"Mm-hmm," Jack replied.

I said a silent prayer that he was taking a drink. Even one drink would do.

"Where is it?"

He was at my side and I nearly jumped.

"The tea for Bastienne. Where is it?"

I hurriedly poured a cup and he took it without another word. I gulped and leaned against the counter.

Jack's cup sat on the table, the chair he'd been sitting in still pushed away from the table. I felt as though I was drifting in a dream as I approached the table and looked over the rim of the cup. It was empty. Jack had drunk the entire cup.

I let out my breath and ran about the kitchen. I quickly dumped the remainder of the tea I'd made for Jack into the sink and rinsed it down the drain. Then I rinsed out his cup, scrubbing it firmly.

I turned the heat on the other tea down, allowing it to simmer on low. It would afford Bastienne at least another few days of relief, if they trusted to allow her to drink it.

Then I sat at the table, hands in my lap and waited for the Water Hemlock to take effect.

It was nearly an hour before I heard the commotion. The startled cries of women. Someone calling, "Jack?" and then a scream.

I didn't wait. I ran through the back door and to the sounds of the horses.

With the amount of light pouring outside from the house it was easy to see once my eyes adjusted. A bank of bridles hung just outside the fence.

I grabbed one, threw open the gate and approached a chestnut mare.

She eyed me cautiously as I approached.

I whispered to her in an effort to avoid spooking her. As I slipped the bridle over her ears and fastened the buckle, I heard a woman's voice screaming for Teddy. And then for Davey.

I pulled the reigns, leading the mare to the fence. With one step, I was up and on her back, kicking her withers to spur her into a running gait.

I'd paid close attention and was certain I knew my way. But where was I making my way to? There was no way I was riding this horse back to New Orleans. But I could get back to Cleric's Cove.

Returning to Cleric's Cove was a stupid idea. Everyone there would give me up in a minute. Hadn't they been hiding Jack all the while? Maybe I could hide out. Gather some food and clothes. I was certain Mo had hidden a gun in the kitchen. If nothing else, I needed to get my knife. I had to try. Something told me that my only true option was in the going to the cabin. There might still be a gun there that would give me a solid chance.

I kept to the road, the horse running as if she knew the way. I checked over my shoulder every few seconds, certain I'd see the lights of cars coming after me. But they never appeared.

The horse galloped through the houses and into the clearing in Cleric's Cove. I pulled her to a stop halfway down the trail, turned her back toward home and gave her a smack, sending her running back the direction from which we'd come. I'd have a far easier time avoiding detection if I made my way through the bayou in a stolen pirogue.

My steps were light on the trail. For once, gators were the least dangerous thing I imagined hiding in the overgrowth.

I hid in the bushes for a long time watching the cabin. There was no movement. I could hear no sound aside from the usual nightly symphony of southern Louisiana.

When I was confident no immediate danger lurked, I slipped from the trees and made my way into the cabin, quietly closing the door behind me.

Even in the dark I knew my way around. I had no doubt I could retrieve the pistol Mo had hidden. It was either on the shelves or in the wardrobe. As I fumbled along the shelves my spirits plummeted. Aside from three pieces of candy, which I tucked in my pocket, the shelves were empty. The gun had to be in the wardrobe, along with the knife.

The air shifted as I stepped through the doorway into the front room. Before I could turn away, an arm snaked around my neck. I was pulled against someone and a hand clamped over my mouth. "Shh," he said.

I stiffened in disbelief. There was no way Jack's men could have beaten me to the cabin.

"Deirdre?"

It was Mo's whispered voice. The hand over my mouth released, and I was spun around by my shoulders so that I faced the figure in the dark.

"Is that you?"

I nearly collapsed in relief. I fell into Mo, wrapping my arms around his waist.

He grunted and pulled away.

"What hurts? Is anything broken?" I whispered.

"Nothing." His hands remained firm on my shoulders. "How did you get away? What are you doing here?"

"I came to get the gun," I said. And then I focused on the current risk. "We have to go. They're gonna come fer me. If they find me, they'll kill me this time. And you as well."

"What happened?"

The reality settled heavily in my heart. I wasn't the same person who'd fled the cabin this morning. I wasn't the same person who had left Cleric's Cove while Mo was being beaten by his uncle's men. I had returned with the dark taint of murder on my soul.

"I killed Jack."

"Let's go," he said.

"Wait!" I scrambled to the wardrobe and threw open one

door. I patted the bottom frantically. Each item my hand travelled across seemed foreign in the dark. Frustration threatened erupt in my throat just as my fingers fumbled against the familiar weight of the handle of my blade. I pulled the knife from the wardrobe and wrapped it quickly around my thigh before joining Mo at the door.

With a soft hand on my back, Mo led me from the cabin and toward the path into Cleric's Cove.

"We can't go there. They were hiding Jack. They let him kill Joseph."

"You have to trust me, Deirdre." He took my hand, and we walked swiftly along the dirt path.

I pulled against Mo as he approached Leonie's house. The memory of her dull eyes as she closed the door behind Jack were fresh in my memory, as was the raw bite of her betrayal. "No way," I hissed at him.

"She didn't have a choice, chér. You don't understand what it's like for them. They depend on the Morets."

"Joseph is dead because of her."

"I trust Leonie. She's always done whatever she can to protect me. But certain things are out of her power, especially when Jack is involved." Mo pulled me behind him as he rapped on a window at the side of Leonie's house.

It was only a minute before Leonie slipped from the front door holding an oil lamp. Her eyes were fixed on the ground as she passed me, avoiding my hard look.

Mo fell into step behind her, pulling me behind him.

We wound our way between the houses and along the shore to an old shed.

Leonie and Mo stopped and pulled aside an assortment of oyster pots, fishing net and buoys. Behind the fishing gear, Mo pulled on a blanket like a magician and revealed an old truck.

"It's been sittin' in there for long time," Leonie said in her hushed voice. "I don't think anyone's even started it up in months."

Mo climbed into the driver's seat, and the mechanical opposition of the engine groaned as he tried to start it.

My hope plummeted. There was no way out of Cleric's Cove. Even if I did manage a way out, Leonie had proven loyal to the Morets. I couldn't give her any hints as to where we'd be going.

Mo got out of the truck and lifted the hood. He felt about with his bare hands, the cast of the moon through a grimy window providing just enough light that I could see him but not what he was doing.

Leonie moved closer, holding the lamp so that it cast light on the engine as Mo worked.

"Try it now," Mo said.

Leonie set the lamp next to Mo and climbed into the truck. The engine sputtered once, ground and then started up.

Leonie slid out of the truck and Mo pulled it from the shed.

He got out and helped Leonie replace all the items they'd removed.

"It don't look the same, but maybe nobody'll notice."

Leonie nodded at Mo. "Be safe."

She looked at me then. I thought she might say something, but at the last minute she closed her mouth, lips pursed and turned away.

"Leonie!" When she turned back to me I pulled my arm back and drove my balled fist into her jaw. "That's for Joseph."

She reached a hand up while she opened her mouth, moving her jaw about to check the motion of it. She nodded at me. "I deserve that."

I pulled the candies from my pocket and reached for Leonie's hand. I placed the sweets in her palm. "For Odi," I said. "She's a good girl."

Leonie nodded and wrapped her hand around the sweets. A single tear worked its way from her eye. Was it in response to the pain of her jaw? More likely it was the guilt she felt at having been complicit in hiding Jack Moret, letting Joseph be killed and Mo beaten.

I climbed into the truck next to Mo, and Leonie stepped aside as we drove past.

I cast one last glance at Cleric's Cove as we drove into the dark. Leonie remained in road watching our departure. A thought occurred to me. One I'd never thought to ask, but now guessed I knew the answer to. "Where is Leonie's husband?"

"She don't have one."

"Then who is Odi's dad?"

Mo cut a quick glance to me and shrugged as if it pained him to say the words himself.

"It's Jack," I said. It wasn't a question so much a sudden realization. I now understood how Leonie could have betrayed Mo at that point. Why she was never really my friend. She could only protect Mo so long as Jack was unaware because she had her daughter—his daughter—to protect.

To Leonie, I was a threat on two fronts. If I was Jack's lover, it minimized his need for her and ultimately risked his interest in providing for her. With Mo's feelings for me, she was losing the protection of the only friend who shared her dependence on, and opposition to, Jack Moret.

I almost felt guilty for belting her in the face. Almost.

CHAPTER

SIXTEEN

MAY 10, 1930

The lights of New Orleans were a glistening beacon of promise, majestic and regal on the horizon. We'd had a long and tumultuous journey since meeting, and the city was our Mecca.

Mo drove us deep into the darkened maze of roads and alleyways of Irish Channel before pulling to the side of the road. "I have a friend. We can lay low for a few days."

We left the keys on the seat, hoping someone would take the opportunity to steal the truck, thereby putting more distance between us and Cleric's Cove.

Our steps reverberated around us as they echoed throughout the abandoned streets. A cat scrambled into our path and I barely managed to contain the scream that leapt into my throat. Though we'd only traveled several blocks on foot, my body ached with the exhaustion of a lifetime's trek.

Mo slowed and peered through a heavy iron gate before leading me through it, across a courtyard and into an alley.

Just as I doubted the wisdom in venturing this far into an alley in the middle of the night, Mo stopped and knocked in a coded pattern on a door.

A small window slid open and a wary eye looked out. "Jesus, Mo! Get in here."

The peek hole slammed shut, and the door swung open.

Mo placed a gentle hand on my lower back and ushered me in. He turned at the inner threshold and searched into the dark in each direction before pushing the door back into place and sliding the lock into place.

"Mikey, this is Deirdre."

Mikey nodded. His stubby, sausage-like fingers wrapped around my hand and pumped in an energetic greeting while he gave me a wide and nearly toothless smile.

Although his welcome was friendly, his attention never truly turned from Mo. "What's up, man?"

"I need to lay low for a day or two," Mo replied, assessing the back hallway of the room we'd just entered. His steps were light as he approached the corner and peered around, craning his neck to look up the stairway.

"Yeah, sure. You can take Mary's room. She's singin' at a club in Chicago for a few weeks. She won't mind since it's you, man."

Mo thanked Mikey and took my hand. He led me through the hall and up a narrow stairway. Nocturnal shadows cast gray, purple and black patterns in varying shades across peeling wall paper. Each step creaked its opposition to our weight as we climbed toward the darkened landing.

At the top step, Mo released my hand. A wooden thump was followed by the metallic screech of rusty hinges as the door swung open.

I followed Mo's shadowed form through the doorway.

His arm waved over his head, grasping, and then he pulled at a chain.

A small bulb hummed to life from the low, cracked plaster

ceiling. Ivory light reached into the darkness but failed to penetrate the darkest corners of the sparse room.

Mo slid the dingy, floral patterned curtains across the window as I stood by the door taking in our accommodations.

Though the furnishings were minimal and simple, the room had a rich and vibrant personality. Several bright colored boas draped across the double bed's splintered cherry headboard. On the far wall, a shelf displayed a collection of cloche hats and beaded headbands. Colorful plume feathers decorated some of the hats, and hair adornments were artfully arranged on a lower shelf.

A hand drawn poster advertising the return of "The Sultry Jazz Styling of Mary Mercier" hung slightly off-center beside the window.

"We'll hide out here for a few days, then I can get you out of here. I'll send you wherever you want to go." Mo poked around in the room, lifting clutter and opening drawers. He pushed aside a blanket that covered the closet and pulled out a large box.

"Send *me*? What about you?"

Mo lifted the box lid and rifled through men's clothing of different sizes and styles. He held a shirt up to himself and draped it over his shoulder before returning the box to the closet. "I told ya before, Deirdre. I'm a Moret. I'm expected to live and die like a Moret."

His family allegiance infuriated me.

Mo turned his attention to the clothes hanging in the closet and tossed a floral-patterned shift dress to me. "Here. Mary won't mind."

I threw the dress on the floor and grabbed Mo by the arm, spinning him so that he was forced to face me. "Mo, did you even hear what I said about Jack? I killed him. And yer runnin' off about what dress I should wear?"

He winced. It was subtle, but unmistakable. "I heard ya."

"There's no way they're goin' ta let me get away. They'll come fer me, and they'll come fer you. Ye helped me get away, Mo. God forbid yer father find out." My voice was just shy of yelling. How could he not anticipate the danger he was in?

He looked at me. The bruises and lacerations that had been only shadows in the car and under the light of Leonie's lamp were now blossoming in full color—purple, black and yellow marbled across the entirety of his face. The smooth pattern on his skin was marred by the tattered flesh of lacerations at his left temple, eye, cheek and his lip.

My anger ebbed, and I was flooded with sorrow for him. That he could accept whatever judgement his family handed him out of pure obligation while they showed no loyalty in return was unfair.

I sat at the edge of the bed. As I spoke, my voice was softer than I'd intended, the secrets were reluctant to be voiced. "Why were they goin' ta let Joseph kill ye? What'd ye done?"

Mo straightened and pursed his mouth as he turned his back to me.

I crossed the room. With my hand placed gently on his cheek, I pulled him around to face me. "What'd ye do to deserve that, Mo?"

"I was weak. Ya can't be a Moret and be weak."

My voice was low and smooth. I held his gaze, so he understood this was an answer I needed him to tell me. "What did ye do?"

"Joseph and a guy named Tully Bishop set up their own business. They was makin' deals with our suppliers and sellin' in Belle Chaise. They thought we wouldn't know. I found Tully, and I made sure he wouldn't ever go against Moret again."

"You killed him?"

He shook his head and leaned against the wall, distancing

himself from me as he revealed his secrets. "Nah. I beat him up. Put him in the hospital for a few days."

My dormant fears about who Mo really was bubbled up. He was capable of beating a man—probably many men—near death, and all in the name of his family. He'd calmly faced down multiple threats in the short time I'd known him. Only a man with the devil on his side would be so comfortable traveling such dark paths, right?

He took a deep breath and continued. "But Joseph was different. He was someone we trusted. He was one of us, and he betrayed us, so his punishment was s'posed to be worse. I couldn't kill him though. I grew up with him. And when I wouldn't kill Joseph, Claude demanded he kill me. It's better to kill his own son than let anyone think he's a pushover."

"Why would ye go to them now?"

"It's my family. They're what I was given in life."

It was this Mo, the loyal one, the one who'd helped me escape from Jack and from his family, that helped chase away the fear I felt about the other Mo. I stepped toward him again and reached for his face, so he had to look at me. I was gentle so as to not press against his injuries, but I was also insistent that he listen to me. I leaned close to him, feeling his heat against me. "*I'm* what you were given."

I pulled his mouth against my own and kissed him softly. Trying to claim him from the Morets. I was determined to claim him as my own, to break him free from the obligation he felt to a family who only viewed him as tool in their network.

Mo hesitated at first and pulled back.

Demanding his body respond to mine, I leaned further into him.

In an instant, his defenses dropped, and he pulled me against him, bringing me more deeply into his kiss.

I clutched my arms around him, pressing my body against his in greedy insistence.

Mo gasped and winced, pushing me away gently. His breaths were rapid, but pain was evident on his face as he angled away from me, arm held tight to his side.

"Let me see." I lifted his shirt and gasped at the purple explosion of color that engulfed his entire left side. "*Oh, Christ,*" I cursed as my fingers trailed the injured area.

I checked for signs of abdominal injury and ensured Mo wasn't having trouble breathing aside from the pain in his ribs that pinched his brow with each breath. In the closet I located a carefully folded sheet stitched with pink and yellow blossoms along the top edge. With the gorgeous linen ripped it into wide strips, I tied them around Mo's ribs to help splint the injury. "I'm afraid there's nothin' else I can do."

"I'll be fine," He reached for me and pulled me in for another kiss.

I melted against him, careful to avoid his injuries. "Say you'll stay with me, Mo."

"I'm with you."

"Promise me." Without a promise, Mo would fall victim to the loyalty that'd been demanded of him by the Morets. They'd use that damn family to manipulate him to his grave. But Mo was man of his word, a man of principles, and once he committed to me—

"Promise me," I whispered against his lips.

"I promise," he surrendered.

SEVENTEEN

MAY 11, 1930

It only took a day of sleeping for me to recuperate, leaving me to feel like a trapped animal.

"Why don't we stay here?" If I couldn't return to Ireland, I couldn't imagine being anywhere but New Orleans.

We'd spent the morning lounging in bed and considering our options. I had no interest in running to Chicago or New York—both were too big. Mo had no interest in heading west. "New Orleans is big enough we might never be seen again. We can change our names. Maybe start a business."

Mo's fingers traced a path from the back of my neck, down my spine and the across to my hip before coming to rest.

"What business would we start?"

"I could start a clinic or do home visits. There's always a need for someone who know how to deliver babies."

"That's a bad idea. Anyone lookin' for you'll look for nurses first."

We came up with—and then discarded—several ideas, the grand as well as the mundane.

"What is something you know a lot about?" I imagined

maybe Mo could repair cars or had some other skill we could capitalize on to get by until we figured out a long-term plan.

"Liquor."

I giggled. "If only we could make a living drinking liquor."

"Not drinking." Mo said. He lifted himself up on one elbow, wincing as he did. He looked at me with a serious expression. "Running, distributing, selling. We're in New Orleans. Most of the liquor bein' run in Louisiana is comin' here."

"We can't bootleg, Mo." I had no idea how to be a bootlegger. "And if they'd come looking for me as a nurse, they'll certainly be on the lookout fer you to be running liquor."

He looked at me and smiled, his eyes alight with excitement. "Not bootlegging. Selling. By its very nature it's a secretive business, not like being a traiteur. We just need a place to set up."

"A speakeasy?"

Mo nodded. "If we do it right we could make enough money to go anywhere we wanted. We could move to Paris in a few months if that's what ya wanted."

"A speakeasy." It was the one thing that actually made sense. The one idea that felt right.

"We just need a place," Mo said.

I slipped from the bed and tossed Mo his pants and the clean shirt he'd pulled from the closet.

"Get dressed. I have an idea."

CHAPTER

EIGHTEEN

MAY 12 TO JUNE 27, 1930

The thick heat of the early afternoon air further weighted the melancholic mood pressing against me as I stood beside Mo in front of the French Quarter home I'd shared with my family.

Dust and sea salt clung to the surface of my happy memories. The once cheerful, yellow paint of the shuttered doors and windows was chipped and peeling. The red brick had the appearance of having been neglected far longer than the five months since Mam turned the key in the lock and pulled me away. A rusted nail secured a sign to the front shutter informing anyone who came within reading distance that the bank now owned the property.

Relief and sadness jockeyed for dominance in my heart at this empty, abandoned and sad reflection of my former life. "Mam and Da couldn't afford the payment anymore. Luckily nobody else seems to have been able to either."

I attempted to peak through the slats of the shutters, but the effort proved fruitless.

"The front rooms are set up for a cafe. Mam tried to earn extra money the best she could when Da got sick. Finn and his

149

friends built a wall to separate the cafe from the parlor. The wall is solid. I couldn't ever hear a thing from the cafe when I was in the house."

Mo appraised the front of the house and the neighborhood in both directions as I spoke.

"There are three small rooms down the hall to the left. Mam left them in case patients showed up. The farthest room has a door that leads to the parlor." As people ran poor and the financial crisis spread, fewer people sought the help of a doctor. Even seeking a traiteur's assistance became a luxury. It was a sad time when people embraced death so their families might be able to afford one turnip for the coming week's soup. Mam had always held out hope that her patients would come back, and she could return to the trade she'd spent her life perfecting.

Mo nodded appreciatively, His initial uncertainty about this dusty old relic gave way to belief in the potential it held. "How much did your parents owe?"

"I'm not certain." My heart dropped. Buoyed by big aspirations, I'd failed to consider the cost of reacquiring my family home. Something in my mind regarded this as my family's house, giving me the right to walk back into it.

"I can find out. I know some people."

"Where will we get the money? I didn't think about that."

"I've got money," Mo said. He pulled me to him and kissed my temple without further explanation. "It's perfect. Right here on Royal Street."

Within two days, Mo knew the exact dollar amount my parents owed on the house, offered the bank a hundred and fifty dollars less and signed the paperwork in my brother's name. He listed me as co-owner. "It should belong to you," he said. "It always should have."

The keys were light in my hand, the weight of freedom and hope. Energy burst from my pores as I threw open the shutters and pulled Mo through the front door. I was excited to share the best features of the house with him, the ones that made it the perfect location for a speakeasy. "The cafe is small and manageable. We can serve sandwiches and coffee. Nobody's needin' more than that these days."

The eatery occupied a small area with a six-seat counter dividing the service area from the dining room. A pass-through provided a glimpse into a back kitchen offering minimal counter space and a single stove. Five small round tables sat along the wide dust-covered window looking out over Royal Street. Mismatched wooden chairs provided seating for two adults per table.

I grasped Mo's hand and pulled him around the corner to each of the treatment rooms. "I don't know what we can use them for. Smokin' rooms maybe."

In the third room I tugged the door of the narrow closet. The upper corner stuck but gave with a second pull. I threw Mo a taunting smile as I stepped inside and pushed against the paneling. It popped open, joints squeaking a bit in opposition to being opened after so long.

Mo's face lit up like a lad gazing up at his first Ferris wheel. He stepped through the doorway into the hidden parlor.

"Made it easier to get away when the difficult patients showed up. Mam could say Da had been called out, and he'd stay in the house until they left."

Mo followed me through the rest of the house. We determined the parlor really was the best place to set up the bar. Mam's piano remained in the room and could provide entertainment. The heavy woven damask drapes would easily block out the sunlight and prevent indoor lighting from being seen by anyone outside of the house. Several of the houses on this stretch of Royal Street were empty and the owners of the others could easily be persuaded—with cash, of course—to mind their own business. Everyone in New Orleans was struggling. A little money went a long way to reduce problems.

"This is the best feature." In the mudroom, at the back of the house, I pointed out the old coal chute. A small hinged door blended into the paneling. Another was located on the outside of the house. "The coal could be brought in without the delivery boys havin' to go through the house. And the owners could get the coal without having to go outside."

Mo pulled the door open and ducked low, looking into the small space.

"Finn used it to stash some of the items he was fencin'. It was also big enough for him to hide in. He reset the doors, so they weren't as obvious. A revenuer might not even notice it. If nothin' else, it's a quick getaway. There's an old shed in the next yard that backs up to it. It has a false wall in the back with shovels leanin' against it. Even if the police went in, it'd take them time to figure out there's a door at the back of it. By then, we'd be long gone."

"Your brother was a natural," Mo said with awe. He cast a quick look at me to see if he'd offended me.

I smiled at the memory of Finn and the ideas I'd thought were ludicrous at the time. "Yeah. He definitely found his callin'. He anticipated everythin'. Almost everythin'."

Mo pulled me against him again and kissed me full on the lips before he turned to survey the parlor again. "Finn laid the ground work. Let's you and I get this place ready for business."

It took a week to simply clear the dust and clean everything in the house.

The bank hadn't gotten around to selling off the furniture yet, I imagined they hoped for a buyer with the money to buy the house and furnishings together. Their optimism had worked in our favor.

I pulled the dust sheets aside and hauled everything out to

the yard. After a decent bit of knocking about, each piece was dust free and hauled back up the stairs into the house.

The cafe was easy to prepare. With the tables and chairs dusted, we polished the kitchen fixtures and cleaned top to bottom. Mo placed a radio in the cafe to play ball games and music. "It'll help cover any other noises that might drift out. And if anyone ever complains about noise, we'll blame the radio."

At night, we slept on the second floor in Mam and Da's old bed. It felt awkward at first as though I was disgracing their memory. Then I remembered Mam telling me about when she and Da moved into his parents' room after they married. Only my grandfather was living at the time, and he refused to let the newly married couple sleep in a single bed when there was a larger one. Mam felt guilty at occupying the bed another couple had shared. "It's the way of the world," my grandfather had told her. "Each generation steppin' aside to ensure a future of new generations."

My own feelings were more likely laced with guilt that I wasn't a different person while occupying my parent's bed. I was now a murderer, preparing to operate an illegal speakeasy in our family home, which I shared with my bootlegger boyfriend. It was no doubt *not* the future my parents once envisioned for me.

I'm sorry, Mam, I whispered as I cast a glance toward Heaven. I offered a quick sign of the cross to prove I hadn't forgotten *everything* she'd ever instilled in me.

June settled hot and heavy in New Orleans, and July was only days away. I dreaded the increasing heat of summer. My skin longed to feel the caress of the early morning breeze that rolled in across Lake Salvador.

The club was nearly ready for business. Mo and I unpacked glasses, wiping them down and sliding them into place on the shelves of our newly installed bar. Mo had negotiated a decent price from a restaurant that recently shut down for Prohibition violations. All the glasses had been hastily packed in newspaper and boxes by some boys Mo hired off the street.

Newspapers littered the pine floorboards of the parlor when we'd finished. It had been months since I'd last heard news that wasn't delivered by word of mouth or focused on Cleric's Cove or the Moret gang. I scanned the headlines for updates as I collected the rubbish for the bin.

A mug shot photo on one of the front pages drew my attention. The headline read, "GRANGERS RAIDED. GANG MEMBER SHOT."

A haunting young girl stared back from the photo, dark and wavy hair mussed and threatening to engulf her face. Her eyes had the vacant, defeated look of someone who'd dared to bet on a single dream, only to have that hope snatched from her. She was beautiful in life, I saw that in her as well as the fire that simmered below the surface of her defeat. The girl's haunted expression as she looked at the camera felt like a warning to me. This could be my future. It wasn't a man on the front page of the *Times-Picayune*. It was a girl.

I read the headline again. I recognized the name "Granger" as the gang that had moved in on Moret business when Claude was jailed. Tim talked about a girl who worked for them. I examined the photo again then read the article.

Her name was Ophelia Breaux. She'd been fleeing from the revenuers when they shot her. The rest of the Granger Gang escaped.

They left her behind.

Several months ago, I might have wondered what could cause a girl to get involved with bootleggers. Now the sobering reality of my own choices settled heavily on my shoulders. I sat at one of the tables in the parlor and quickly found myself lost in the gaze of Ophelia Breaux. I tried desperately to hear any message she might convey to me. We were nearly the same, weren't we?

And she was left behind.

"What are you readin'?" Mo entered carrying another box. He sat it on the table and looked over my shoulder.

I handed him the paper.

When he finished the article, he placed it back on the table, picked up the box and carried it to the bar.

He didn't turn. Over his shoulder he said, "You can get out of this if you want. It's prob'ly for the best actually. What happened to that girl, that's real, Deary."

I pushed myself up from the table. Every possible response flitted through my mind as I bridged the distance between us. He'd given me a way out. What we were doing was dangerous —and illegal. I could end up sitting on a cold concrete bench next to the girl from the Granger Gang. How long would I even last in jail? Did I really have it in me to be a criminal?

I leaned against the bar beside Mo.

Caution tempered his gaze, and his breath grew shallow.

"I don't want out of this, Mo. We're doin' somethin' of our own here. This place, everythin' that's happened for us to get this. It means somethin'. It means *everythin'*."

He nodded.

"Besides, this happened nearly a month ago. It doesn't affect us at all." I looked at the article once more before forcing myself to throw it away.

Mo nodded and pulled me in tight against him.

Our preparations were complete, and we were ready to open in early July. We settled on Independence Day, both for the potential revenue from revelers flocking to the city, as well as for the significance of the holiday. Mo and I had our own business. Nobody in Cleric's Cove knew where we'd gone. We were no longer at the mercy of Claude Moret.

I was wiping down the cafe counter when a man pulled up out front in a truck. The truck's paint was faded denim in color, with rust serving as the dominant color tone. Ragged holes speckled the body, seeming to have been eaten away by splattering of acid.

Mo met him at the bottom step and led him down the hall and into the meeting room. From there, I knew they'd be heading into the club.

I burned with curiosity but gave Mo the time to make whatever deal he might be working on. I poured a glass of sweet tea and sat at the closest table to the door, facing the hall. I might give him the chance to make a deal, but I'd also be sure he didn't think he'd get away without telling me about it when he finished.

When they came out again, I got a better look at the man. His hair was dark as night and closely cropped. His skin was as richly colored as a man who spent each day toiling in the sun. He looked up and his caramel eyes regarded me as no more than a nuisance. There was no guarded reaction to my presence, he seemed to have no reaction to my being there at all.

My nerves jangled in anticipation. Danger radiated off him and filled the air as he passed. I had no doubt he'd turn on a person at any minute just for being in the wrong place. His wide, sturdy frame nearly brushed both sides of the doorway as he passed. While Mo was strong and muscular, he was far more lithe than this man. I wondered how I could have ever found Mo dangerous.

"Who was that?" I asked as his truck rattled to life and drove away.

Mo sat across from me. I slid my tea across the table, and he took a drink. "He's gonna be our distributer. Our first delivery'll be here before sun up."

"How do you know that man?"

Mo thought for a moment. He rubbed his palms into his eyes before he looked up. "That's Eloi Granger."

"What?" How could Mo trust our liquor delivery to the gang who'd always been his family's main rival? "How could you bring someone in here who hates you? He could tell Claude where we are."

Mo reached across the table for my hands. He held me so that I had to listen to him. "Eloi Granger hates Claude, and he hated Jack. There ain't nothin' in the world he'd ever do to help one of them. Including tellin' my dad where I am. He's the one person we *can* trust to not give us away."

His reasoning seemed solid, but it still seemed dangerous to trust a Granger. Especially with our opening only days away. And I couldn't erase that girl's photo from my memory.

They left her behind.

"I have somethin' for you. Come on." Mo pulled me by the hand. He closed and locked the front doors then led me into the smoking room.

He reached under one of the leather chairs and pulled a package free. Faded twine secured brown paper around the parcel. "I hope you agree."

"What is it?" I settled into a chair and tore at the wrapping.

"A sign. For the club, or the cafe. Whichever you prefer."

We hadn't discussed signs, or even a club name. I couldn't imagine why Mo suddenly found it so important that it become a gift.

By the weight and feel, I knew it was made of wood. The rise and fall under the paper hinted that it had been chiseled. I peeled the paper away and was stunned into silence. I could neither form—nor think of—words to express the emotion that flooded through me. I stared gape-mouthed at the sign that lay in my lap. My fingers trailed over it as the burn of emotion pinched at each side of my nose. An emerald green base offset gold painted and raised letters that read "FINNIGAN'S END."

"That was it, wasn't it?" Mo asked. He knelt beside me and held the sign up, so we could both see it better. "It was Finnigan's End. Not Connall's End?"

I smiled recalling the fib I'd told him the morning as we'd sat on the front porch of the cabin, watching the rain fall. Had it only been two months ago?

"This is beautiful. I think it needs to hang behind the bar where nobody can touch it." There was nothing I could do to save my brother, but this one memory of him—and every other Finnigan who'd led me to this moment—would be cherished and protected as much as I could protect anyone.

While Mo hung the sign, I slipped a record onto the old Victrola we'd purchased—from another closed violator. I was eager for the club to fill with customers. I marveled at the transition from a plain family sitting room to a sexy speakeasy. Heavy plum-colored velvet curtains partitioned off some of the tables to allow for a perception of privacy amongst our future clientele. A crystal, tiered chandelier hung from the copper ceiling tiles in the middle of the room. Rich wood tables complemented the mahogany bar. Candlelight flickered and danced across the table tops from the crystal cups Mam had saved for the afternoon teas she'd never hosted.

It was perfect.

Mo slipped his hands around my waist, and we moved in time to the slow raspy sounds of the trumpet and bass that drifted from the speaker and filled the room. The bump and scratch of the needle against the record provided a subtle underlying rhythm that our bodies fell into tempo with. I turned into Mo, moving in time to the music, swaying with his body.

"I have one more thing for you," he said. He stepped back and reached into his front pocket. As he pulled his hand out, he knelt on one knee.

Balanced between the tips of his thumb and first finger was a ring. Tiny square emeralds framed a marquise shaped diamond. The jewels caught the light from the chandelier overhead and sparkled brilliantly. Each point of the diamond was aligned with Fleur De Lis patterned gold. A patina finish provided evidence that the ring had been owned—and loved— by someone before me.

"Deirdre—" Mo stammered. His brows pinched tight, and he looked up at me and whispered, "What's yer middle name?"

"Fianna," I giggled.

"Deirdre Fianna Cassidy, I don't know what I ever did right

in my life that brought you into it. I do know that I'd be dead if you hadn't come along. Will you let me spend the rest of my life trying to repay you?"

I nearly crammed my finger into the ring and dropped to my knees in front of him. "Yes. Of course."

Mo pulled me into a deep kiss. Clutching me to him.

I wrapped my arms around his neck and leaned back, pulling him to the floor with me. Desperation ignited within me and I yearned to feel him against me. My legs slid around his hips and I lifted myself against him until he sank on top of me.

The pressure of Mo's body only intensified my craving for him. Grasping at the back of his shirt, I pulled it over his head. Mo's kisses paused long enough for him to escape his shirt and then began a slow trek along my neck and décolletage. Electricity shot from each tenderly placed kiss along my collarbone. My body writhed in ecstatic anticipation.

As each button of my dress was sprung free, Mo traveled further down. An eruption fluttered low in my abdomen as the heat of his kisses reached my navel. A moan slid from between my lips, carried on the draft of my wanton gasps.

Mo's hands slid under my dress and traveled up my thighs.

He stopped at the same instant I felt the tug of the band around my thigh.

"Can we make love for once without the knife being within reach?" Mo asked. He pulled it from my leg and tossed it over his shoulder.

A clatter erupted as the knife struck glass, and all fell to the floor behind the bar.

Mo's eyes were wide. We both looked to the bar then back to each other.

I was determined to not be interrupted though, and reached for Mo, sitting up to meet him as he raised to his knees. My hands grasped at his hips, and I lifted my chin to look into his eyes.

Mo's pupils were wide and his gaze intense, fixed on my own as if he could absorb me at any moment.

A breath caught in my chest and fought for space against the hammering of my heart. My shoulders blazed with heat as Mo's fingers brushed against them, pushing my dress until it slid to the floor. Freed from the confines of my clothing, I wanted nothing more than to feel the heat of Mo against me. With one arm, I pulled him back into me, while my other hand pushed frantically against his waistband to free him even further.

The dazzling sparkle of the chandelier cast twinkles of light that danced across our bodies as we immersed into each other and our licentious impulses.

IT WAS four in the morning when our delivery showed up.

Mo and I had just swept away the last of the broken glass. The steps were heavy on the back stairs. With no time to slip the knife band in place on my thigh, I tucked it beneath a stack of dish towels under the counter.

It wasn't Eloi Granger that brought the liquor, but two of the delivery boys who shared his dark, rich coloring. I assumed these boys to be related to Eloi. The youngest was barely into his teens. His smile was the friendliest smile of anyone I'd come across in months. Just being in his presence made the room—and the world in general—a happier, more hopeful place. It was a rare gift to carry such a life light in dark times.

The older brother—what had Mo said his name was? Remy? —seemed preoccupied. He barely acknowledged we were there. He simply carried in the liquor, set it down behind the bar and returned for another load.

Before they left, Mo shook the hand of the black man that was with them. "Thank you, Sunshine."

The man nodded. "You let Eloi know when you need another delivery."

They stepped through the back door and were absorbed into the night. If It hadn't been for the boxes and bottles of liquor piled around the bar, I might have thought I'd imagined their entire visit.

Mo and I stood beside the liquor for several minutes.

I mentally inventoried every bottle and jar, calculated how many drinks we could sell and how much we planned to charge per drink. Every plan we'd made, every bit of preparation we'd undertaken, had brought our dream to fruition.

Mo and I looked at each other, smiles breaking across our faces. We had liquor. We were ready to open. Finnigan's End was about to become a reality.

TWENTY

JUNE 30 TO JULY 1, 1930

Business at Cafe Cassidy was slow. A few men began to gather mid-mornings to sip chicory while arguing over whether Hack Wilson or Babe Ruth would end the season with the most home runs, and a far more contentious argument, if Lou Gehrig would surpass both.

Kids of all ages popped in periodically for a Coca-Cola, nickels clenched in their sweaty palms and faces flushed from heat.

I didn't mind that business was slow, it was only ever meant to be a cover for the speakeasy in the back. But seeing Mam and Finn's hard work put to use made me happy.

Mikey, from our first night in Irish Channel, came to work in the cafe. His friendly demeanor would bolster the image of a friendly diner, but his size would ensure nobody started trouble from the front of the house.

Mo and Mikey installed a buzzer. A switch under the counter in the cafe would ring behind the bar should trouble present.

I minded the cafe counter as they put the finishing touches on the bar.

We were ready to open the doors to Finnigan's End that night. A full three days early.

Mo invited people he knew from around New Orleans, offering them three days of special access. He reasoned those people would help spread the word about Finnigan's End and July fourth, our official opening night, would be a bigger success.

The list of tasks that still needed to be completed occupied my thoughts. Though I saw the woman on the sidewalk pause and look through the window, it wasn't until she took to the steps that I really took notice of her.

She was out of place in the afternoon foot traffic. The sunlight cast a shine across her licorice-colored hair. Perfectly crafted finger waves gave way to loose curls that softly skimmed her shoulders.

Kohl defined the almond shape of her dark eyes, sweeping up dramatically at the edges to give her a feline appearance. Her flawless skin was naturally tanned and offset by precisely painted crimson lips.

My eyes were drawn to her deep red dress. Narrow pleated straps capped her delicate shoulders and dropped into a deep V between her breasts. The wrapped bodice fit snugly while the skirt skimmed across her curves, swaying with the sultry swing of her hips as she walked.

Black ribbons crossed each other around her ankles holding impossibly high heeled shoes in place.

She didn't have the look of someone in the mood for a sandwich or a cup of chicory coffee.

"Can I help you?"

She smiled. Her eyes appraised me as mine had just done to her.

I tugged at my sensible shift dress, suddenly overwhelmed with inadequacy. I'd deluded myself into believing the delicate floral pattern made the dress as pretty as it was functional.

She glided to the counter and slipped onto the nearest seat. Her voice was silky and her speech a near-ideal representation of Southern charm. "I believe I'm here to help you."

"Do I know you?"

She laughed and held a hand out. "I don't believe we've been introduced yet. But I'd like to think we're already friends. Seein' as how you're wearin' my dress."

I gasped. "You're Mary! I'm so sorry. Mo said you wouldn't mind."

She laughed again, holding firm to my hand and patting it to calm my panic. "Don't you worry. That color looks far better on you than it ever did on me."

She sat straight, pulling her shoulders back. "I'm Mary Mercier. And you're Deirdre?"

"Uh...yes. I'm sorry. I wasn't expectin'..." I stopped. It was far better to stand mute than continue to stutter unintelligibly.

"Mikey mentioned you may be in need of a singer, and my schedule is currently wide open."

I recalled the poster on Mary's wall. Mo and I hadn't considered a singer, but the idea was phenomenal. What was a speakeasy without a sexy songstress?

Within the hour, Mary had joined Mo and I in the club. She polished the mirrors and helped with one final dusting of all the tables before excusing herself to "tart up" for her performance.

A bartender and two doormen, friends of Mo's, ambled into the cafe shortly before sunset. Mikey led them in and introduced them to me.

"She's in charge. You do what she tells ya," he warned them before returning to the cafe.

As the sun set, the clamoring of my nerves increased. Our success—or failure—would be determined within the hour.

Although it wasn't the official opening, I couldn't help but feel this would be the night our future would be gauged by.

Entry into Finnegan's End would be a tiered process. A few of Mo's trusted contacts had been given a password for direct access through the back door. Others would enter through the cafe and comment on their desire to have a cigarette while considering the menu. After being directed to the smoking room and ordering the appropriate off-menu item from the attendant—a Bayou Etoufee—they'd be granted access through the hidden panel.

The coal chute would serve as an emergency escape route should the revenuers show up.

"Just make sure you're out first," Mo had warned me.

Dusk passed into darkness, and Mo sat on the front steps to help guide our guests when they arrived.

As I waited to greet the first customers, I stood behind the bar with Dutch, the bartender. My knuckles ached from my constant wringing of my hands. Several times I looked over my shoulder at the sign hanging behind the bar. The gold lettering that spelled out FINNIGAN'S END glistened in the low light of the darkened club.

The glow of the candles and the few bulbs along the bar reflected in the mirrors and crystal chandelier, causing a magical speckle of lights to glimmer throughout the room.

Dutch slid a glass of brandy in front of me. "A nip'll help with the nerves. Always does."

I offered him a grateful smile.

The fair skin of his scalp reddened beneath the thin cap of snow white hair. His narrow eyes jumped away from mine, and Dutch pushed his small, wire-framed glasses back up his flat nose.

Mikey had assured me that, despite his general nervous demeanor, Dutch was the best bartender in New Orleans.

Mary was the first to arrive. She sported attentive men firmly attached to each of her arms. A wiry young man—distractedly shuffling sheet music—trailed behind.

While the young man settled into place at the piano, Mary sat the men at the nearest table. She made a show of lavishing attention on each of them before coming to the bar. She slapped bills on the bar top. "Gimme three of anything. The tall one's buyin'."

Dutch poured two fingers of moonshine into three glasses.

I leaned toward Mary and whispered, "Who are they?"

She cast a glance over her shoulder before turning back to me and shrugging. "Thirsty."

With a wink, Mary tossed back one of the drinks and left the glass on the counter before delivering the other two.

Dutch raised his brows and shook his head at me as he retrieved Mary's glass and submerged it into the sink of soapy water.

Within minutes of Mary's arrival, more customers began to trickle in.

Piano music and boisterous talk filled the room.

I was rooted in place as my family parlor transformed into a working speakeasy before my eyes.

"Go on, lassie," Dutch encouraged me, indicating the crowd of people looking about the room.

I eased from behind the bar, taking a deep breath. "Welcome to Finnigan's End, ladies and gentlemen."

Mary and I made the rounds, assuring each table had drinks and our attention. Although the men were flirtatious, they seemed to know I was Mo's girl. Their flirtations with Mary were far more daring, their comments bordering on salacious.

Confident in her own role, Mary handled her admirers expertly. She managed to tame even the most rambunctious with only a few words, while her flirtatious demeanor kept them engaged and wanting more.

I continued to visit each table, my presence was no match for Mary's, but I knew the importance of establishing myself as a proprietor and ensuring my customers were happy. Of course, in the midst of Prohibition, it didn't take much more than a plentiful supply of spirits to meet that goal.

"You're a natural."

I hadn't noticed Mo enter the club, but his warm hand on my hip and the whisper of his breath along my neck brought my focus firmly back to him.

"It's everything we planned, isn't it?" I replied.

We stood in the middle of the club, our hands entwined, bodies leaning together as all around us the reality of our dreams played out.

Men and ladies gathered around tables. Plumes of smoke rose, and the bitter aroma of cigarettes and cigar smoke drifted throughout the parlor. Clear and amber liquids sloshed in glasses as they were transported from the bar to tables, sometimes splashing on to wood or down the front of clumsy drinkers. Laughter and the cacophony of boisterous conversations filled the room.

Mary began to sing, and the smoky tone of her voice seemed to entrance everyone. Conversations became whispered and a few of the men sat, enraptured, as she swayed and purred one song after the other.

"Everything," Mo agreed.

TWENTY-ONE

The official opening of Finnigan's End was an even greater success. Word spread throughout Vieux Carré, and Finnegan's End became the most popular "secret" on Royal Street.

Within weeks, we were turning people away. People would loiter in the cafe, buying sandwiches, coffee and colas in the hope they'd get into the club should someone else leave.

"We need to hire more people," I told Mo.

It had never been our intent that Mikey would be actually running a busy diner, and Dutch could barely keep up with drinks.

Within three weeks of opening, we had two employees for the cafe, and a bartender, server and bar-back for the club.

The Grangers made a fresh delivery in the early morning every Thursday. Both Remy Granger and Sunshine proved guarded about discussing their own family. Even Sirus, despite a strong penchant for pralines, was difficult to coax information from.

I did learn that the girl from the newspaper, Ophelia, had been Remy's girl, or *gaienne*—Mo kindly translated the unfamiliar Cajun term. In mid-July, when Remy didn't accompany Sunshine and Sirus on the delivery, I learned that Ophelia had been released from jail.

Relief swept through me that the girl with whom I had so much in common with was finally free. That she'd be fine after all. Some part of me saw this as proof that I, too, would be okay.

But she wasn't a murderer, I chastised myself. I shook away the dark reminder, choosing to focus on the present.

Each morning, in the hour after Finnigan's End closed its doors on the last customer, Mo and I counted our earnings and divided it between the house fund and envelopes for each employee.

"We can make that trip to Paris now," Mo said, shaking a stack of bills in my direction.

I snatched the money from him and tucked it into an envelope. "No, sir. We aren't about to leave this place just yet. We're just gettin' started. There'll be time for travel later."

Mo became still. "And when are ya' gonna marry me?"

I started and looked directly at him.

Uncertainty cast a shadow across his eyes.

We hadn't discussed marriage since the night he'd proposed to me. *Did he think I meant to not marry him after all this?*

My left thumb traced the band of my ring. "I'll marry ye today, Mo Moret. Right now. Do ye doubt me?"

A smile crept across his mouth. "Nah. I don't doubt ya. Just wanted to make sure."

On the last week of July, the Grangers failed to make their delivery.

Mo phoned several times, but there was no answer.

"We have plenty of liquor to last a week, maybe two." Despite my attempts to reassure Mo, he became more distracted.

He spent most of his time by the front door, looking up both sides of the street as if he anticipated something. Mo reached out to his contacts in New Orleans and Belle Chaise trying to find out why the Grangers had suddenly gone missing.

Within days, he had an answer.

We were awakened early in the morning by someone beating on the front door.

Mikey's face was ashen as he passed a newspaper to Mo. "You need to lay low," he said. "The law's lookin' for everyone named Granger or Moret. There's a bounty."

Over Mo's shoulder I saw the headline of the *Times-Picayune*: GRANGER GANG AND MORET GANG AT WAR. JUDGE KILLED IN THE CROSSFIRE.

Mikey ran a hand through his hair. "There's more, Mo."

His pinched gaze lifted from the paper to his friend.

"I got word this mornin'. From someone in Plaquemines Parish. Remy Granger's dead. Ambushed."

My heart collapsed into itself. I thought of that girl again. She'd been spared from jail only to lose everything in the end?

Mikey continued. "The youngest one too. And Eloi's girl got beat up. She's real bad off."

Buzzing filled my head, attempting to drown out any more of the horrors Mikey was relating. That entire family had been brought to its knees.

Once again, the reality of every risk I was taking in my own life became glaringly clear. Maybe it was a perfect time for a trip. Mo and I could get away and give this feud time to subside. "We should go. Now."

"Nobody knows yer here, Mo. Nobody that's talkin' anyhow. This is the safest place for both of ya."

After hours of debating the risks of staying or leaving, it was decided we would stay in the house for a few days to ensure no Moret members were lurking about in the neighborhood waiting for us to try and slip away. Neither Mo nor I would go into the cafe nor into the club during business hours. We spent the next four days quietly ensconced on the second floor with the windows covered and lights dimmed.

Mikey delivered food and drinks several times a day. Nobody else seemed to know where we were.

Each night, we sat in the dark listening to the lively sounds from the club we could no longer be seen in.

I looked forward to our early morning reprieve when Mo and I would sneak into the club to clean up from the night's revelries. With the receipts counted, pay distributed, and club tidied, we'd retreat to our darkened confines.

"We can't keep livin' like this," Mo said after six nights in hiding.

It was Sunday, the only day of the week Finnigan's End was closed. We'd spent the entire afternoon in the parlor. Cleaning and polishing was far preferable to hiding out upstairs.

"In the mornin' we cash out. We leave Mikey to run the place."

I looked around the club. It was as rich and vibrant with energy now as it was with memories of my family. The thought of leaving tore at the depths of my soul.

With a nod of agreement, I stood and began to walk through the club, saying silent goodbyes to every corner where memories lurked. Even though I was resigned to leaving my mind clambered for an excuse to stay.

I trailed my fingers over the cool ivory keys of Mam's piano and forced the tears to remain at bay. There was no time to break down now. And this life of mine was no life for cryin'.

"Well, ain't this somethin'." Claude Moret stood at the door. A sinister smirk spread across his face as he sauntered across the parlor and leaned against the bar.

Two large men stepped through the door and remained just

inside the doorway. That route was effectively gone as a means of escape.

The men were even larger than Claude Moret. They both wore faded tan button-up shirts—maybe they had been white at one time? —with perspiration stains spreading lower as they stood in the heat of the room. Their hair was oiled back, but sweat beaded along their hairlines, causing them to look as though they'd just stepped from a rainstorm.

In the hallway behind them, I noticed the shadowed presence of at least two other men and my heart dropped.

TWENTY-TWO

Mo remained calm. He continued to wipe the glass in his hand with the towel. His eyes cut to me, but only long enough to see where I was. I was certain he was trying to avoid drawing attention to my presence. His voice was controlled as he asked, "Can I get ya a drink?"

Claude picked up a bottle of the Granger liquor and inspected it. He reached across the bar and chose a glass, filling it near full with the crystal liquid. He lifted the bottle, taking a deep smell. He held Mo's gaze and then let the bottle slide from his grip.

The glass jug clattered to the floor, collapsing into itself against the wood. Shards of glass skittered along the ground. Liquor splashed across the planks, darkening the wood grain and clinging to the face of the bar.

Claude looked at his shoes, shaking one at time to kick away the droplets that clung to the top of each foot.

He lifted the glass in a toasting motion and took a deep pull of his drink. He swallowed loudly and set the glass back on the bar. "Ya didn't hear I busted out, eh?"

"I heard," Mo said, ignoring the mess his dad had just left.

He remained calm by all looks, but I detected a tempest of fear brewing under the surface. Whereas I could only imagine the things Claude Moret was capable of, Mo had seen—and even experienced—some of the most atrocious acts his father had perpetrated.

Claude looked around the room. His face pinched in distaste as he took in the club. "And yet, here ya are, hidin' out in some half-rate speakeasy."

He turned and looked at me. One corner of his upper lip pulled up, exposing the enamel of his browning teeth. "With yer murderous immigrant whore."

Mo reached across the bar, scrambling for a grasp on his father.

"No, Mo!" I scrambled across the room, desperate to stop him, to pull Mo back, though I knew I hadn't a hope of doing so.

Claude slipped just past Mo's grip, and his men swarmed.

One grabbed me around the waist and pulled me back as three descended on Mo.

I fought against my attacker, kicking and lurching in an effort to break his grasp. My efforts were futile. He was twice the size of me.

As we reached the other side of the room, he flung me into the tables. Tables and chairs scattered and splintered as my body bounced off them.

The impact of hitting the floor drove the breath from me. I tried gasping in response to the pain, but my lungs refused to cooperate. My eyes bulged as I struggled. Finally, I drew a gasping breath and pushed myself up to lean on a hip with my legs curled to the side.

The men who'd attacked Mo were still driving blows into his face.

Another man lingered behind the bar, inspecting and then

dropping bottles and glasses. The clatter of broken glass filled the club.

The man caught me looking at him and lifted a beautiful pitcher. My father had received it from a particularly grateful politician whose wife nearly died in childbirth.

I knew immediately that I'd failed to disguise the importance of the pitcher in my expression.

One corner of his mouth tucked into a sardonic smile, and he raised his brows questioningly as he lifted his arm higher, then released the pitcher.

At that moment the shattering glass no longer had an effect on me. It was only glass and booze.

"That's enough," Claude finally commanded his men.

Mo remained on his knees. Though he swayed, he would give no indication that he was in fear or pain. His expression remained neutral.

"How'd ya think this was gonna work, boy? You's just gonna run off to N'awlins and start yer own business? That I wasn't gonna care? That I wouldn't be comin' around for my cut?"

He laughed a deep and diabolical laugh as he took slow steps, circling Mo.

"That ain't how it works in our fam'ly now is it, *Junior*?"

Mo said nothing. He didn't even look up as Claude paced around him. He stared defiantly forward, his mouth tight in a snarl of fury and humiliation.

I couldn't tell if Mo was as terrified as I felt.

Claude spun and, grabbed Mo by the hair and drove a knee into the side of Mo's head.

The crack that emitted from the impact stunned and sickened me. I called out involuntarily in surprise and opposition.

Mo collapsed on the floor.

Claude pulled his foot back and drove a kick soundly into Mo's belly.

Mo didn't move.

"Stop," I cried out. It came out as more of a demand than I'd intended.

The man behind me yanked my hair, causing my back to arch. I reached up with my hands, trying to stabilize his hands, to reduce his impact on me. He drove me backward toward the ground.

I tried to scream, but only managed a garbled eruption.

Sharp pains erupted in my lower back and I was forced to bend my knees and follow the path of his pressure until I was sitting on the floor. He pushed me forward until my forehead nearly touched my ankles. A counter pressure lifted up against my throat, as if a garotte was being pulled against my neck. My breath became a wheeze, fighting to pass the constriction of my throat. Circular bursts erupted in my field of vision, black spots across a horrific reality.

The thin pressure dug into my skin, I recognized that he was using the chain from my locket to strangle me. The pressure in my head intensified, and I clutched desperately at the chain, trying to wedge my fingers beneath it to make just enough room for a breath to pass. My skin was swollen against the pressure of the chain, and my fingers far too large to get a grip on it.

After everything I'd done to avenge my family, I realized it was my solitary tic to them that would be my undoing. I should have burned the locket in the barrel with the photo. The image filled my head again, Mam, Da and Finn, the corners bubbling and burning in the orange embers of the fire. I focused on them, willing them to be there to greet me when I crossed to the other side.

In that instant, the pressure became too much, and the chain snapped. The release was miraculous. Blood pounded back into my head, and a sharp sting of air passed through my raw and damaged trachea.

I cried and couldn't stop myself. The pain and fear collaborated against me to topple the brave demeanor I'd crafted.

The pressure on my head eased and as I lifted up a bit, I saw the boots that stood before me. Claude Moret's boots.

"Let her up."

My assailant pulled up on my hair.

I was forced to scramble to my feet for fear the hair would be ripped directly from my scalp.

Claude leaned directly in front of me as I was pulled to standing. His crooked nose nearly touching my own. His breath was hot and smelled of too many cigarettes washed away with too much coffee and the bitter hint of a whiskey aftershot. "You're the little Mick bitch that killed my brother."

There was no way I'd answer that question. It wasn't really a question any way. Simply a statement of a fact that we both knew to be truth.

Claude slipped behind me and shoved. His hands, firm on my shoulders, forced me to within feet of where Mo swayed quietly on his knees. "What I don't know is what you're doin' with Junior. You makin' yer way through the Morets?"

I shook my head, fear churning in my belly.

He crooked his finger and pulled my chin at a painful angle so that I was forced to look him in the eyes. His voice was soft and dangerous. "I ain't had my turn yet."

His men laughed.

A pit opened up in my stomach, and I felt as though I'd be swallowed into it. At that moment I trusted having his "turn" would be the least horrible thing Claude Moret might do to me. I'd killed his brother, run away with his son, and started an illegal business with one of his rivals as our supplier. Moret could, quite likely, ensure my last hours on earth were filled with every imaginable horror. And he would do so without the knowledge that I'd intentionally insinuated myself into his circle with the sole objective of destroying him and his family.

I realized even with the amount of trouble I was currently in, I'd seen my goal through to the end. Moret's business was practically crippled, Claude was a wanted man, his family was in tatters, his brother dead—at my hands—and his son had more loyalty to me than to his own father. If I died now, I would have accomplished the vengeance I'd set out for. Even if I'd only been a witness to most of it, my very presence had spurned some the outcomes into being.

But I wasn't going to go willingly. There was no way I'd beg Claude Moret for my life, or for leniency. I would plead for Mo, but I knew that would only cause him more pain. If Claude knew how deeply I loved Mo—or how Mo felt about me— he'd use our feelings against us.

I chanced a glance to where Mo kneeled on the floor. Shards of glass were scattered around him and pinpricks of blood covered his arms and the knees of his pants. His gaze was steady, though I saw his relief that I was okay—for now. His expression betrayed no hint of what he was feeling or thinking.

I gave him a slight nod. *We're in this together.*

A blow to the backs of my legs caused them to collapse beneath me, Claude forced me toward the floor.

I assumed Mo's expressionless demeanor as I sunk to my knees facing Mo.

Claude paced around us. His slow gait carried him between and around us.

Mo and I remained immovable forces.

Claude accepted my necklace from the man behind me. He held it up to the light for only a few seconds, curiosity focusing his attention to the round locket that swung lazily from his thick fingers. He slipped the chain into his front pocket without another indication that it was anything other than a curious trinket.

"You really fucked ev'rythin' up, Junior. Course, I knew ya didn't have it in ya. I shoulda let Jack kill ya when he wanted to. Joseph sure as hell couldn't get it done."

I nearly betrayed my knowledge when my body gasped in response to his harsh words. Jack was going to kill Mo? By this point I shouldn't have been surprised by anything the Morets did, but I'd never get over my disgust at how they could treat their own family. Their *children.*

"And now I hear yer settin' up shop with them Grangers. Well, what's left of 'em."

My heart pounded. I cast a look to Mo. *What actually happened to the Grangers*?

Claude caught my expression, laughed and retrieved his whiskey from the bar. He threw back a deep swallow then ambled to where we kneeled on the floor. He grabbed the back of one of the chairs as he passed and dragged it behind him. His pace was unhurried, and the chair legs stuttered and emitted a low whine as they scraped across the unpolished planks. Claude spun it around and kicked one leg over, sitting on it so that his thick chest and belly leaned against the back of the chair. He took a sip and drew air in between his teeth as he shuddered against the burn of the moonshine.

"Them Grangers do make a fine liquor. Shame they ain't gonna be makin' anymore." His maniacal laugh returned, and he looked over his shoulder to his men, who stood awaiting instructions. "Alcide here said that youngest one screamed like a girl when the first bullet went into him."

Waves of revulsion rolled over me. I could only assume there'd been others, by the reference to a "first bullet". I remembered the boy. His dark curly hair and sweet, genuine smile would forever be etched into my memory.

"All the other bullets didn't faze him much, did they, Alcide?"

"Nah, boss. He din't seem to notice none of the others."

I swallowed the horror that crept up. These disgusting men had callously ended a pure life simply because they'd lost some revenue.

"Eloi Granger ain't gonna be in our way either. The message we sent him was clear." Claude stood again, circling us then stopping in front of me.

I remained immobile when he reached to stroke my cheek with his fingertips. My jaw betrayed me and shuddered against his touch.

Claude's voice dripped with tainted sweetness. "It's a foolish man who lets his love for a woman be used against him. I truly felt bad for what we did to Eloi's gal. She was pretty."

He offered an exaggerated shudder, as if it took some great effort to shake the displeasing memory from his mind and stepped away. "But maybe it wasn't her looks Eloi loved."

At the table Claude took another drink then set the glass aside and ambled to Mo. He pulled him by the hair and bent over. His teeth were bared as he growled in Mo's ear. "There ain't gonna be no more Granger liquor in here. Ever!"

Claude stood up and looked around as if taking it in for the first time. As if finally appreciating the opportunity he'd stumbled upon. "This is my place now. And I'm supplyin' the liquor. And I'm takin' the cut."

"Like hell," Mo growled.

I wanted to shush him, to yell that if Claude wanted the place we'd walk out right then and there. I was done holding onto the past. He could have my parents' house, the club, and everything we'd set up. It was only stuff, it could be replaced. Mo was the only thing I wanted to walk out of here with. We could disappear into the night. Find some place where Claude would never come looking. Even a position as a tenant farmer sounded preferable right about now.

Claude's face pinched in question. "Are you telling me my business, *Junior*?"

"I'm tellin' you this ain't yer place." Mo's voice took on a dark and ominous tone I'd never heard before. He'd reached a level of darkness I feared might soon consume him. The same one I'd reached before I killed Jack.

I was determined to save Mo from that stain on his heart. "Let him have it, Mo. It's not important. There's far greater things than this."

Mo's eyes were dull as he looked at me. With everything that had been taken from him, and everything he'd endured at the hands of his family, he'd never dared to dream of anything beyond them. Right now, it must seem as if he was losing everything he'd thought possible.

I had to let him know that none of this mattered. If we had each other, we would have everything.

"What do you mean there's more?" Claude leaned forward in his chair, looking directly at me.

Through gritted teeth I answered. "There's more important things than this club, or yer liquor. Things ye can't take from us, no matter how ye try."

"Is that so?" An acerbic grin engulfed his face.

My hair was firmly entangled in Claude's grasp, and I was pulled off balance before I'd even seen a movement from him. I was thrown to my back and dragged across the floor.

"No!" Mo lunged to his feet.

The two men in the doorway remained steadfast as the two in the room met Mo with fists and kicks. The blows echoed throughout the room.

"Deirdre!" Even while fending off the blows that rained upon him. Mo was focused on me.

Claude's breaths were heavy as he drug me past the bar.

I grasped at the corner, holding steady with all the strength I could muster.

A tortuous ripping sensation pulled at my head as Claude yanked backward in an attempt to free my grip. I held even tighter, my fingers burning in opposition to the effort.

With a savage yell, I let go and lifted my feet, rolling on my back until my feet were positioned within striking distance of Claude's legs. Channeling every bit of strength I possessed I kicked at his shins and knees.

"Bitch!" He exploded.

But the surprise loosened his grip, and I scrambled away from him.

His hands grasped at me again, vice-like on my hips as I ran behind the bar.

I lunged but couldn't break his hold. My fingers grasped at the bar, trying to find leverage, but only meeting the weight of partially filled liquor bottles.

Mo's yelling gave way to grunts as Claude's men continued to beat him. He'd been driven back to the floor and I doubted he'd be able to fend off the blows much longer.

Desperation finally gifted me with some degree of clarity. With no great attention to my aim, I picked up a bottle and tossed it over my shoulder in Claude's direction. I felt him sway to avoid it.

I launched another. And then another.

He cursed and lurched, dragging me as he did so.

I continued my assault until, finally, the *thud* of a bottle of Granger hooch was met with a sudden release in his grip. I spun around, just as Claude shook off his surprise and focused on me.

Rage pulled his lip into a snarl as he lunged for me.

Not daring to turn away from him, I grasped frantically at

the shelves behind the bar. My fingers were met with a heavy, solid weight. I gripped the Finnigan's End sign with both hands and swung like Babe Ruth.

The impact of the sign hitting Claude's head reverberated through my entire body. My teeth ached, and a sharp pain traveled from my elbows into my shoulders.

Claude fell to the floor without a sound.

One of the men attacking Mo turned his attention to me just as the two in the doorway finally turned, realizing things were not going as expected.

As one of Mo's attackers ran toward me I ducked behind the bar, hiding seemed my only option.

A glint of metal caught my eye as a meaty hand slid around my arm. I allowed the man to yank me upright and from behind the bar, the momentum carrying my left hand and the knife it grasped.

I looked him in the eye as I drove the blade into the soft underside of his jaw.

His eyes registered awareness just as the blood began to pour around my grip. He coughed against the flow as I pulled the knife free and he slid to the floor, lost in his own struggle with mortality.

I turned toward Mo. He was no longer moving, but the rotund man continued delivering kicks to his abdomen, back and head.

The two men at the door had entered the parlor and were hesitantly moving forward. My odds were growing worse with every passing moment. I was alone. Against three men.

Without a plan, or so much as a thought I leapt onto the back of Mo's attacker. A scream burst from the depths of my chest as I struck him in the chest with the knife. I withdrew the blade and drove it into him again, this time with an intentional blow to the neck. He fell without another purposeful movement.

Sticky crimson blood covered my hands and splattered my arms and dress. I held the knife in front of me and screamed at the last two Moret men.

They paused looking to each other for confirmation—or confidence.

I screamed again, baring my teeth in the most feral way possible.

The men, hands up, backed from the parlor and through the door. Their footsteps thundered as they ran through the house and out the front door.

I stood for several minutes, blade shaking in my hand as I held it, pointed at the doorway.

Mo moaned, the sound of his breath against fluid reached my ears. Blood trickled from his mouth and nose.

I quickly assessed him and rolled him onto his side. His breathing was clear, but he wouldn't wake up.

Behind me though, Claude Moret also began to moan.

It took only a few minutes for me to locate several lengths of rope I'd set aside when we were preparing the club. But Claude was a big man. How could I effectively secure him so he couldn't get loose?

I rolled Claude onto his side and laid a chair over on the floor and pushed it behind him. Starting with one side, I lashed his wrist, then ankle to the chair. With great effort I managed to roll him onto his back, the chair rolling into place underneath him. When I'd tied his other arm and leg to the chair I realized the difficulty I'd face in lifting him, but I knew with a man as powerful as Claude, if I didn't secure him better he'd easily break free.

I struggled, but couldn't gain enough leverage to lift the chair upright.

I considered killing Claude where he lay, but I'd never be able to get the body out on my own. My only option was to bind him in place until Mo could help.

Claude's head lolled as I wove another bit of rope from the backs of his legs, around his neck and through the structure of the chair.

Wiping the sweat from my hands and brow, I secured his upper body to the back of the chair then scrambled back to where Mo lay.

"Please, Mo. Wake up. I need ye, luv." I shook his shoulders gently, but he didn't respond.

Claude on the other hand began to make guttural noises and pull against his bindings. His eyes remained closed, but it was only a matter of time before he woke.

I had no desire to be caught alone with Claude Moret.

TWENTY-THREE

I scrambled into the cafe. My hands shook like a sot recovering from a bacchanalian weekend.

The faint glow of late afternoon sun wasn't enough that I could clearly read the wall. With the blade clutched in my right hand, I used my left fingers to travel along the numbers Mo had written on the wall. Which was the one I needed?

Mo had a long list of connections in New Orleans, and it seemed he'd written every contact number he had on the wall. I cursed myself for not paying better attention when Mo added each number to the wall. I knew that none would be listed by true names. There'd be some sort of code, something to indicate exactly who each number belonged to that no other person—particularly law enforcement—would recognize.

My finger crossed one that had been hastily scratched in pencil. *Grocer PP 1127.* The door to a memory flew open: Eloi Granger owned a store in Plaquemines Parish.

That was it. The only other person who hated Claude as much as Mo did right now was Eloi.

I lifted the receiver.

A tinny voice was on the line. "Number, please?"

"Plaquemines Parish 1127." I struggled to control the quaver in my voice.

"Hold, please."

A jangling erupted through the ear piece. And then another. As the third ring clattered unanswered my desperation grew even more frantic. My impulse was to drop the phone and run back to the club. I didn't trust that Claude hadn't somehow risen from unconsciousness and broken free of his binds. That was just the kind of evil that he was.

A fourth ring.

This is ridiculous. There's no way he's goin' to answer. Even if he does he won't come all the way to New Or—

"Breaux's." The greeting was abrupt. Not so much a word or greeting as it was a bark of acknowledgment.

I knew right away that it was him.

"Eloi? Eloi Granger?"

"Who's askin'?"

"My name's Deirdre. You delivered—I mean we met in— we met with Mo. You're the grocer." I wasn't sure how exactly to call his memory to the fact that he'd delivered moonshine to our club without really saying it. I'd heard of phone lines in New York being listened in on by revenuers. I couldn't imagine the state of Louisiana had gone to that great of an effort yet, but if they had, the Morets and Grangers were at the top of the list of bootleggers they'd be interested in listening to.

Even without wiretapping I couldn't risk piquing the curious nature of telephone operators.

"I remember."

"I need—"

He interrupted me without giving me a moment. "You're gonna have to find someone else. I ain't deliverin' no more."

"It's not that." I had no idea how to say it gently, so I tried the direct approach. "I was told that ye might like to finish a conversation with...with Claude Moret."

"Who told ya that?"

I dropped my voice to a low mumble. There was nobody around to listen except for the operator. Claude was unconscious and bound. Mo was unconscious. Two of Claude's men were bleeding on the floor of my club. "I have him here. He's a little, um, *tied up* right now. In the other room."

"Mo can take care of him."

"They beat him up. It's bad. He hasn't woken up." Desperation pushed tears into my eyes. My throat threatened to constrict. *Be calm, Deirdre.*

"Eloi, it was Claude. Yer brother and yer girl. He said as much."

"I'm on my way."

The line went dead.

I was left alone as the evening began its slow descent over the city. Fear kept me rooted in place.

The sound of kids venturing into the shadows of the buildings to play in the streets echoed from outdoors. From a distance, the muffled sounds of music slowly drifted through the summer air. Musicians along Bourbon Street ambled from their daytime hibernations to play long into the night.

The hot day was giving way to the sultry nights of New Orleans. Soon the streets would fill with revelers. Where the heat of day had driven the people indoors, leaving behind quiet streets, the night would bring some gaiety and boisterous summer fun.

Perfect, I thought. The crowds and noise, as well as the general chaos of a New Orleans summer night would make it easier to do what I knew was coming. I'd have to get rid of two bodies, likely three before the night was over. There was no way Claude Moret could be allowed to walk out of Finnigan's End alive. He'd never allow Mo or I to walk away from this battle with our lives.

I comforted myself with a dark satisfaction. I'd made the right call, with Mo unconscious, Eloi Granger was the one other person who could help me face what I had to do. Before the night was over, I'd have one more murder obscuring any light that remained in my soul.

With a deep exhalation, I forced my nerves to calm and mind to focus.

I retrieved a length of twine from behind the cafe counter and tied it snugly around my thigh. *Careful*, I cautioned myself as I slid the blade into it.

The shutters were heavy as I swung them across the front door and windows. They echoed with a finality as I pulled them together and slid the lock into place.

I crept along the hallway. The house felt dark and ominous, as if evil spirits lurked around corners that didn't even exist in this straight passage. My ears strained against the silence, searching for any indication of danger.

I turned into the third room. My fingers lifted the hem of my dress and my hand wrapped about the handle of the blade at my thigh.

Claude looked up as I entered. Even in his current position, tied to a chair at the back of an empty club, he was not giving up. The Morets were resilient if nothing else.

Claude's head lolled as he grinned. A dark red stream poured from his swollen and purple lower lip.

"I'll give ya one last time to do what's right, girlie."

I pulled myself up straight. I was determined that, despite the panic churning inside me and causing my stomach to tumble and my heart to pummel against the confines of my ribs, I'd never again let Claude see me afraid of him. He was bound like a pig on a spit, and there was nothing more he could physically do to me or anyone else. "I believe I am doin' what's right, Mr. Moret. Perhaps we 'ave differen' opinions on that though."

I pulled a chair closer, though my unconscious impulses ensured I remained out of reach. Vengeful though I may be, I wasn't completely stupid. As I sat, the hem of my dress hitched over the handle of the blade.

Claude noticed it as well. He looked from the blade to the bodies on the floor then back at me. His expression was almost prideful, as if it brought him a level of joy to see that I'd killed his men. "They had families, ya know."

I reached to lower my hem from the knife, then changed my mind. Instead I smoothed out the material around it as if I was proud of the blade and confident with having it. I raised my eyes to meet his. "As did I."

His brow furrowed. He had no idea who I was or how I came to be in his circle.

A dark pleasure filled me. My heart lightened more than I'd felt in months.

Guilt flickered in my mind, warning me of the risk of taking joy in my actions. I pushed it away. This was my chance to destroy Claude Moret. And, before he surrendered physically, I'd destroy him with the truth. The truth of how a "filthy immigrant whore" had infiltrated his family, killed his brother, and beguiled his son. I'd also tell him everything I knew about the Moret enterprise and planned to the revenuers.

I leaned back in the chair, reaching for the half-full glass of moonshine Claude had left sitting there.

The liquor burned a path over my tongue and down my throat. It settled in my belly, warming me further. "My brother worked fer ye. He went missing five months ago. I promised me mam on her death bed that I'd find him. And that if I found anyone to 'ave hurt him, I'd get vengeance fer 'im."

"I don't know yer fuckin' Mick brother," he growled. He jutted his chin forward and struggled to sit up straight and defiant against the ropes.

I smiled at the futileness of his efforts.

"But ye did," I took another sip, careful not to shudder in response to the harsh bite of the alcohol. "Ye left 'im as collateral fer some of yer associates. As I hear though, ye had no intent on coming back fer him. Just left him there."

A deeply satisfied grin engulfed Claude.

He knew who Finn was, he remembered and imagined that knowledge would somehow set him free. Claude thought he could use his typical means of getting control of the situation, but I wasn't about to be manipulated by him.

"I ain't the one you're *en colaire* with, *Beb*. It was him." Claude jerked his head toward where Mo lay in an attempt to redirect my fury to someone else.

Mo moved just a bit but remained unconscious. His breaths worked heavily against the collection of blood in his mouth. With one look, I knew that his breathing was steady and that he was okay.

I shook my head and offered Claude a sad smile. "*You're* the one I'm angry with. What happened when Mo tried to rescue Finn wasn't his fault. It all rests on you. And, you may not realize this, but I've just about finished everythin' I came here for."

A laugh erupted from him. "You ain't done nothin'. You think because you got me tied to a chair right now that this is over?"

His anger took over, seeping into the controlled facade he'd crafted. His voice raised, nearly a yell. "This ain't over. I may be lyin' on the floor like a dog now, but when I get loose—and I *will* get loose—I'm gonna take that blade from your milky little thigh, and I'm gonna skin ya with it."

I raised the glass slowly to my lips. Swirling the crystal liquid before I took another sip. "Yer not gettin' loose. I tied ye meself. A little somthin' I learned ta do as a girl."

I returned the glass to the counter and scooted the chair even closer to Claude, dangerously close. Toying with him was instilling in me a feeling of power I'd never felt before. Even when I took the life of Jack Moret, I hadn't felt the satisfying power I did in that moment. A dark swirling tempest had overtaken me, like demons lifting my soul and carrying it into the darkest lair of hell. "I want ye to know what I've done. I want ye to die with the knowledge of what exactly happened." I leaned and whispered, "I want ye to know that everythin' came about because of me. Because of what ye did ta me brother."

"Deirdre?" Mo coughed and moaned as he shifted.

"Ya better check him," Claude taunted.

I cast a look to Mo, but I wouldn't let myself be distracted from this moment. "I found yer brother and I followed him. I learned everythin' I could about him—and you—and then I made sure he saw me. I enticed him, lured him, and teased him until he brought me to Cleric's Cove. Then I waited and listened. I learned everythin' I could about yer business. And I'm goin' ta tell the Marshalls everythin' I know about you and Jack. I'll tell them about yer bootleggin' business, and yer whorehouses, and the names of everyone yer associated with. Your whole business is done."

He sneered. "You do that, and I'll take that weak excuse of a son down with me. Are you plannin' on him goin' ta jail too?"

I smiled sadly at Claude and cast a look to Mo.

He'd started to push himself up from the floor. One hand to the side of his head. I imagined it was either the pain or dizziness slowing him.

"He's not goin' to jail because you won't be tellin' anyone anythin' after tonight."

"You plannin' ta kill me?"

I raised my brows in thought. "I killed yer brother, didn't I?"

His face crumbled as he realized the degree of danger he was actually in. For once in his life, Claude Moret wasn't in charge and didn't have much hope of regaining the upper hand.

"You poisoned him. Do you got it in ya to kill me one-on-one?"

I considered his question. It was a fair one. It was one I'd considered before I ever made the call. I nodded and leaned in his direction conspiratorially to whisper, "I do have a friend. He's quite interested in havin' words with ye. He should be here soon."

Mo croaked from behind me. "What did ya do, Deirdre?"

"Trust me." I knew his concern. Who could we ever trust to walk into the room, where two men lie dead on the floor and one tied to a chair, and not be appalled?

Mo grunted as he struggled to stand.

I left Claude and helped Mo up and onto a chair before getting wet rags to help clean him up and hold against his wounds.

His pupils were dilated.

I'd already anticipated his concussion.

It'd take a bit of time before his thoughts could catch up to what was happening. He grabbed at my shoulders and pulled me toward him. He whispered, "Who's comin'?"

"You have to trust me, Mo. I didn't know how to do this m'self. I was worried ye wouldn't wake up."

"Who?"

I leaned and whispered in his ear, "Eloi Granger."

All the tension Mo had built up let go in one breath. He nodded his head as he slumped back into the chair. "I need a drink," he croaked.

Claude demanded information, barking questions at us.

I ignored him as I tended to Mo.

Mo pushed himself straighter. He wiped at his eyes and shook his head periodically. He was preparing. Though he was resigned to the fact that I'd called for help, he wouldn't show weakness when Eloi showed up.

Shadows settled heavily in the parlor, rendering the room nearly dark. At the bar, I struck a match and lit two candles. I left one there and carried the other to the table near Claude.

He cursed and kicked at me, trying to move the chair along with him.

Mo stood, hands clenched into fists at his sides. His voice thundered throughout the room as he yelled, "*Ça va!*" *That's enough.*

The heavy steps of Eloi Granger were as unmistakable as his large lurking presence. Even the room seemed to hold its breath as he lumbered into the parlor.

Without a change in his expression, Eloi surveyed the area. Though his eyes traveled over them, he didn't register surprise at the bodies on the floor or Claude Moret tied to a chair next to them.

I thought his mouth nearly curled up in pleasure when he looked at Claude.

I stepped toward Eloi, but Mo's arm reached across me and with his hand on my hip he stepped in front of me.

Eloi glanced over Mo's shoulder at me. "She okay?"

He was asking if I'd been beaten as bad as his girlfriend had.

"Yeah." Mo nodded.

A heavy silence descended on the room. Mo and Eloi looked at each other and then both looked to Claude. A silent communication developed between them, and I wasn't a part of it.

Fear flickered in Claude's eyes for the first time but was immediately smothered by the self-righteous anger that dictated so much of his personality. He thrashed against the confines of the ropes and rocked the chair. "I will fucking kill you both!"

Eloi and Mo looked at each other. They both nodded.

Eloi lifted the chair, and Claude with it, into an upright position.

Mo turned to me. "I need you to turn on some music. Wait in the cafe." He pushed me gently toward the door.

I shook my head; I couldn't let Mo do this. His aversion to hurting people had been the very reason he'd been ostracized from and abused by his father. I'd killed; my soul was tarnished. I was ready and willing to do it again to save Mo that burden. "Mo, let me do it."

He used more strength as he pushed me the last step through the doorway into the smoking room.

Behind him, Eloi circled Claude, looking down at him. He was an animal circling its prey.

"I got this, Deirdre. I need to do this." He stepped back and grabbed the door. His eyes were sad but resigned when he closed it between us.

The lock clicked as it slipped into place. It was followed by the heavy rub of something being pushed across the floor and against the door.

Claude's angry voice failed to carry clearly through the door, but the dull thud that silenced him did. As did all the ones that came after.

Numbness overtook me, creeping throughout my body and up into my head. My thoughts and emotions dulled. There was no more fear or anger.

I trekked along the dark hall and into the cafe.

A hum filled the room as I clicked the radio on and adjusted the volume so that music rattled against the counter top.

Even with the shutters in place I felt exposed in the dark of the cafe. I slid a small table in front of the door. With nothing left to do, I sat on the floor, back against the wall and breathed deeply, too tired to even wash the blood from my hands.

While I felt some relief at knowing the threat of Claude Moret was going to be behind me, I felt trapped in the depths of a hell I'd created, and I'd brought that hell into my family home.

Even with a speakeasy set up in the back, this house was essentially unchanged from the day my family bought it. The house had seen so much, our good times and our struggles. It had been there through Da's death and stood strong when Mam and I retreated from it with nothing to our names. It had welcomed me back and housed my vengeful aspirations. But suddenly, I knew I couldn't stay here. While the house was essentially unchanged, I was not. The tarnish on my soul was thick, and every day I spent in this house would serve as a reminder of how far I'd fallen from the person I was.

This house would always be a symbol of every evil and dark thing I had succumbed to. I could never outlive my guilt when the ghosts of an innocence past would dwell here beside me.

It was time to say goodbye to the last segment of the past. My last bastion of hope. Every dream my parents had—except for Mams' dream of avenging Finn—was lost forever. As was I.

The sun rose in a languid pace over New Orleans.

Silence hung heavy in the cafe. I'd flipped off the radio when the streets emptied. For the past two hours I'd listened for tell-tale sounds from the parlor. It had been nearly an hour and a half since I'd last heard anything.

Exhaustion had taken over, and I could no more drag myself down the hall to investigate than I could speak Latin.

All my muscles had long ago stiffened as I'd sat waiting, but I didn't dare move to release their tension. My eyes burned dry from my steadfast attention for any sign of trouble through the shutters.

The door from the parlor creaked as it opened.

I pushed myself to my feet, groaning under my breath as I straightened my aching joints.

Mo walked around the corner. His injuries had turned purple and black, but he'd obviously washed the blood away. As he limped toward me I saw the skin of his knuckles were broken open again, the right middle one actively bleeding as he wiped it against his pant leg. What stood out to me, though, was the haunted look in his eyes.

He pulled me into him and held me tight. His chest lifted with ragged breaths and heaving sobs he was trying desperately to control.

I stood there, questions exploding in my head, but content to exist for just a few minutes without either of us having to explain or think about everything that had evolved in our lives.

He pulled back and I looked up, my questions unspoken, but clear.

"He's gone," he said. "They're all gone."

I followed Mo back into the club. His steps were ginger, and he clutched his arm to his right side as he walked.

Eloi Granger stood against the bar finishing a drink, a half-empty bottle clutched in his other hand. The amber liquid sloshed in the glass before disappearing into his mouth. He set the glass hard against the counter, let go of the bottle and wiped his mouth with his sleeve. Eloi's knuckles were broken open as well. His hands were colored in the same swirling pattern of red and purple as Mo's.

He met my gaze in the same forthright manner I'd come to expect from him. There was no show of guilt, nor acknowledgment he had anything to feel uncomfortable about. He nodded once then looked at Mo. "I don't expect there's a reason I'll hear from ya again?"

"No." Mo shook his head.

They nodded at each other and Eloi slipped a brimmed hat on his head, walked past us through the back door. As it opened, I saw an old truck had been backed up outside.

I looked around the room. Blood stained the floor, two large spots where Claude's men had died. One where Mo had lain after being beaten. Dark maroon speckles stained the floor around where Claude had been seated. The chair he'd been tied to was splintered. A force had been strong enough to drive him against the back of the chair and break the wood in several places.

The images that filled my mind were clear and vivid. I had no doubt as to what Claude had endured. Only one thing wasn't evident.

Mo walked behind me and wrapped his arm around my waist as I surveyed the rubble that had once been our biggest dream.

"Is he dead?" I couldn't take my eyes from the stains.

Mo didn't answer. He shifted and reached into his pocket. He withdrew his hand and held it before me. Pinched between his fingers, my locket spun freely on its chain.

I reached under it, letting the swaying locket brush against my palm before I wrapped my hands around its cool familiar shape.

"The one thing you can't live without," Mo said.

"No. It's not the one thing after all." I leaned against him.

He pulled me tight against him. He leaned his head to touch mine and whispered, "It's over."

TWENTY-FOUR

SEPTEMBER 19, 1931

The salty tang of the ocean air seeped into my pores.

I inhaled deeply, pulling the familiar breeze deep into my being.

On the horizon, the navy sky surrendered to an orange glow and then the yellow burst of sunlight exploded from behind the land across the sea.

"I didn't think it was possible that the sun could be so different here." Mo slipped behind me, his body warming the chill of the ocean air from my skin.

I leaned back against him. "I told ye everythin' would be different."

He laughed and nuzzled deep in the crook of my neck. He placed one kiss and then followed it with several more along the length of my shoulder.

The electrical shudder of anticipation ran its course along my spine. I spun to face him, pressing firmly into him, melding my body to his. "Are ye happy though? Do ye ever regret comin'?"

He was serious as he looked deep in my eyes. There were no lies between us anymore. No need to disguise the worst of ourselves. We were intimately aware of the best and worst of each other. Both extremes had helped define our short time together.

"You know I don't regret anythin'. We got no need for regret. It ain't gonna ever do anything for us."

I pulled him into a deep kiss.

Hours of frank discussion brought us to the realization that we'd made decisions based on factors we couldn't control. Everything we'd done had been to ensure our own survival. We wouldn't allow each other to feel guilty for surviving or for doing what it took to ensure we'd survive together.

The one regret that did haunt me was leaving the house. We didn't just leave it behind though. Every gallon of gas I'd poured on the floors had been a cleansing of the good as well as the bad. I'd reduced my entire past to cinders in the strike of a match. We'd watched from down the block as Finnegan's End burned.

Tears poured from my eyes. I'd finally cried for Da, Mam, and Finn. I'd cried for the Deirdre who'd only wanted to heal people and had instead claimed three lives by her own hand.

"I never imagined it'd be like this," Mo said. He watched the sun rise across the Irish Sea as we did every morning for the last thirteen months.

I turned back so that I could watch it as well. "I promised ye you'd never seen anything like the light at Finnegan's End."

With my husband's arms wrapped around me, his hands absentmindedly traveling across the swollen girth of my belly, and I knew that everything that led us to this moment had been worth it.

And I'd do it again to get right back here to this moment.

Without regret.

Acknowledgments

I'm eternally grateful to the following people: As always, I owe a heartfelt thank you to my family for their love, support and belief in my dream. The Sinner's Club (Clint & Dana Eddy and Nick & Amanda Nelson) for your support, friendship, and encouragement. My brother-in-law, Kevin, who has become the single busiest distributor of my books in the western states. I don't know where you've taken all those books, or who you've given them to, but I appreciate your marketing efforts.

The Louisiana Department of Tourism for always answering the phone and my random questions. The wonderful people at the Barataria Preserve for fielding all the questions I didn't call the Department of Tourism about, and for giving me a bit more specific information about the wonderful ecosystem and history of your region. James L. Weaver, a dude who writes one hell of a crime thriller, but isn't afraid to beta-read romance. You have a great eye…maybe you should write a romance next?

Kelly Risser for helping me polish this novel, for putting the commas where they belong and removing all the others that I'd randomly thrown in. Emma Wicker for ever-so-nicely telling me to watch for the boring words, where those words were, and how to find them myself (Whew, there were a lot!). Coca-Cola for fueling my creative process. The Sweeplings and The Vespers for the perfect mood music! Everyone at Changing Tides Publishing for believing that bootleggers can fall in love too. And a special thank you to everyone who read A Shine That

Defies the Dark and asked me (sometimes relentlessly!) when I was going to write "the next one".

About the Author

Jodi is a YA & NA writer, black belt, registered nurse and case manager for a busy home health agency. She lives with her husband, three sons and an evolving herd of undisciplined animals in Colorado. She has a well-earned fear of bears, but tolerates the Teddy and Gummy variety. She has been obsessed with books, both reading and writing them, for most of her life and prefers the written word to having actual conversations.

www.jodigallegos.com

ALSO BY JODI GALLEGOS

RUM RUNNERS SERIES

A Shine that Defies the Dark, book 1

The Light at Finnigan's End, book 2

THE HIGH CROWN CHRONICLES

The High Crown Chronicles, book 1

Queen of Ruins, book 2

The War Of Myths And Mortals, book 3

Thank you for reading *The Light at Finnigan's End*; I hope you enjoyed my book!

Want to be the first to know when I release new books? Here are some ways to stay updated:

- Sign up for my Email list so you can find out about new releases.
- Like my Facebook page.
- Visit my website: jodigallegos.com/

If you loved *The Light at Finnigan's End*, please tell your friends about my book and consider leaving a review. Reviews are like potato chips; you can't ever have enough of them. Thanks for reading my book!" ~Jodi Gallegos

www.ingramcontent.com/pod-product-compliance
Lightning Source LLC
Chambersburg PA
CBHW032016050726
47590CB00006B/2199